SANGITA SAIKIA

REDGRAB books
redgrabbooks.com

Title : Of Forbidden Attractions
Author : Sangita Saikia

Published By
Redgrab books Pvt. Ltd.
942, Mutthiganj, Prayagraj, 211003
www.redgrabbooks.com
contact@redgrabbooks.com

Printed and bound in Manipal Technologies Limited, Manipal, Karnataka
Paperback, First published by Redgrab Books Pvt. Ltd. in 2021
ISBN : 978-93-90944-48-4
Copyright © Sangita Saikia 2021
Printing rights reserved : Redgrab Books Pvt. Ltd. 2021
Cover design and Typeset in Redgrab Books arts

To Santosh,
For being there.

Acknowledgements

Heart felt thanks to my father for my love of books. He was the guiding light throughout; from whom I had learnt the basics of the language. Thanks to my family for their kind support. A big thanks to Alakesh Baruah for helping me out.

CONTENTS

CHAPTER 1

Celebrations filled the air in this very middle class household and excitement of the otherwise boredom filled souls permeated the ambience of this house. The mundane affairs of life were replaced by the surreal in as many years as one can remember. For the Bharadwaj household was solemnizing the marriage of one of their sons. Nitul was getting married to his college mate, Priya.

Nitul's cousin, Sanya Bharadwaj arrives to attend the marriage. Sanya's mother accompanies her daughter to attend the wedding. Sanya is resplendent in a yellow silk sari and traditional jewellery. She lets her auburn coloured hair loose which falls up to her shoulders. Sanya, her quiet self, often merged into the environs of the setting she found herself in. Raging beauty did not define her. Hers was a more subtle, understated beauty which hinged on anything close to austerity. Beauty was austere; not her inner persona which was full to the brim and threatened to overflow into a flood of emotions if anyone even touched its rim. Also that she was highly opinionated hid behind the veil of silence she preferred to maintain on various matters.It was also her shyness that came to the fore every time the occasion arose for her to express her views.

Today, Sanya is enjoying the sights and sounds of the ongoing marriage celebrations. She watches the bride decked in all the fineries making her way towards the sacred fire to be with her groom and to be tied to him for life in a sacred vow. The bridegroom looks at his radiant wife-to-be and is thoroughly pleased at the prospects the future would bring forth. The expectant bride and groom look at each other in perfect understanding. Sanya, watching the growing affection between the couple, inwardly craved for such a union with another and this perhaps had taken some indistinct form in her mind space. Sanya hoped that her aspirations would see the light of day and she would be elevated to a new state of happiness.

The bride and the groom walked around the sacred fire seven times and sat down. The priest who presided over the marriage asks the groom to put the mangalsutra around the bride's neck. Nitul carefully puts the mangalsutra around Priya's neck and hooks it. Nitul's sister brings forward the little box holding the sindoor and holds it in front of her brother. Nitul takes a small amount of sindoor from the box and applies it in the parting of the hair on Priya's forehead. Amidst the chanting of mantras by the priest, the marriage ceremony concludes leaving everyone happy. The newly married couple takes the blessings of the elders in the family. A sumptuous feast is laid out for the guests after the wedding ceremony is over. The guests savour the delicious food laid out under the temporary shamiana built for the wedding ceremony. From afar it is a jolly, merry making crowd but as one comes near one could feel the simmering tension that beset almost all families. All the relatives of the bride and the groom belong to nuclear families. In the marriage ceremony there is a coming together of these nuclear families. They gather together to celebrate the marriage of one of their own. They are outwardly smiling and happy. The bitterness lie within; in their smugness over their wealth, achievement and social standings and the other's non possession or little possession of it. The distaste of the ones who were lower down the social ladder at the supercilious attitude of the ones above them could not be concealed even on a day as happy as this one. The differences were too ingrained to be swept aside by a day of celebration. The non acceptance of the ones who had newly climbed the social ladder by the ones who had reached there before only succeeded in getting the contempt of the younger and restless lot. Restless for achievement and restless for acceptance.

Arshan Wadia completes his routine regimen at the gymnasium which is fitted out in the ground floor of his huge mansion. Arshan gets dressed to play the role of Chairman of the billion dollar company he heads; a role he plays to perfection. Born into one of Mumbai's well known industrial families, Arshan has donned the role of Chairman since last three years. The title sits on his shoulder as a crown befittingly sits on the head of a bona fide emperor.

Suave, well dressed and well mannered, Arshan Wadia always made a statement whenever he entered a room. Today he enters the boardroom of his office with a steady step but with excitement writ large on his face. Arshan is excited with the prospect of the takeover of a British company in the United Kingdom by his own company. He enters into serious discussion with the members of the board regarding the takeover. He spells out the modalities which has to be adopted during the negotiations for the final acquisition of the company. Intricacies of the process of negotiation aroused his passion.

Passion to reign in business, the steel business, ran inherent in the family. It's like the obsession of the serial killer, out in the shadows, who is ready to pounce on his next victim. As the victim of a serial killer is caught unawares so the companies are in the dark when they are upstaged by one of the Wadia family. Arshan unknowingly but surely had inherited the family trait. The love for the business was what moved the family of the Wadias. But something more than love, something which leaned towards the ruthless defined Arshan's urge for his business. Ruthlessness towards his counterparts makes him a bit of a scary character, whose moves are difficult to anticipate and therefore cannot be foiled. His ruthless nature and clinical precision was widely perceived in the business world.

Arshan leaves the boardroom happy and triumphant as he had been able to bring all the board members around to his point of view. Every member had given their concurrence to Arshan's move to take over the British company.

CHAPTER 2

Sanya is joyous at bagging the internship at the Tata Institute of Social Sciences in Mumbai. She had completed her post graduation in Economics from the Benaras Hindu University which is located in her hometown in Varanasi. The period of internship was six months and she had gained her parent's permission to shift to Mumbai. Sanya is excited at the prospect of newness entering her life although in the inanimate form of a city. A city animated by the zeal of its people and the expressions of their many varied aspirations. A city brought to life by the motion of its people and vehicles; all moving in the direction of their destinations. Mumbai never seemed to halt even at night but seems to be in movement at all times. Sanya would be catapulted from the sedate and certainty of the city of Varanasi to the fervent and uncertainty of the city of Mumbai. She knew as much; she also knew that she was herself ardent enough to merge into the manic city of Mumbai. Mumbai was to be her home now at least for the next six months. She was ready to embrace the new experiences which was very clear to her would be vastly different from her life in her hometown of Varanasi. Varanasi, situated on the bank of the river Ganges, is one of the holiest cities for the followers of the Hindu religion. The many pilgrims, that visit the city and take a dip in the Ganges, believe to have their sins washed away by the holy waters of the river Ganga.

Varanasi, in sharp contrast to life in Mumbai, had the essence of a quiet life. The city's soul being stirred only by the devotion of the pilgrims who visit the place. Otherwise it is a silent city flowing everyday with a steadiness being adhered to by the people who inhabited it. Sanya had lived all her life in this atmosphere. Her life was all but a humdrum existence in this decorous city.

Sanya was the eldest of the three children in the Bharadwaj household. Her father Suraj Bharadwaj taught in a local college in Varanasi. Sobha Bharadwaj, Sanya's mother was a housewife. They were a family of five including Sanya's sister and brother. A family which found solace in their closeness to each other. The love which emanated from the Bharadwaj household enveloped every member in a cocoon. But to an outsider it was hardly visible as every member in this family found it hard to express love in expressible terms but would rather feel its intensity towards one another. They were envious of people who could express their love to others in every carefree and spontaneous manner possible.

Sanya's sister, Meera, was studying engineering in a local college in Varanasi. Meera was outgoing and exuberant unlike her elder sister. Both the sisters, though apart in their tastes for things life throws at one and in their outlook towards life, were attached to each other by a closeness brought about by the familiarity of circumstances they found themselves in. That was one part of it. The other part is the closeness brought about through familial bond. Meera, though the more unreserved of the two sisters, was underneath her skin a conformist. She was most likely to follow the norms of societal constrictions. But not Sanya. Sanya was a bundle of rebelliousness below her cool and calm exterior which seemed to mask an ever churning and energetic mind. Sanya is definitely the non conformist in her family. Societal norms would not stop her in her tracks. She would go all out to achieve her goals – whether emotional or otherwise. Sanya was courageous to the hilt. Her courage, like the tides at sea, would be displayed at times when required just as the tides which rises only in certain circumstances.

Akash, Sanya's kid brother was yet to show off his character or rather his was a half baked character. Looking at him, one could not judge the outcome of the development of his character. After all he was studying in the eight standard in a local school in Varanasi. It was still early stages to mark his character with indelible ink. It still had to go through the rigours of time and the varied circumstances of growing up. He was the kid of the family. His likes and dislikes were often marred by the grown up members of the family.

Sanya's parents had a quiet bonding. Their relationship was born out of understanding and trust. One could decipher the others mind only with a glance at one's face. Sanya was often attracted to this aspect of her parent's relationship. She very often secretly wanted to have a relationship with the man-in-her-life akin to the one her parents have. That is one of deep love and absolute understanding. Sobha Bharadwaj was a beautiful woman, delicate and small built. Her family lived in a lane close to the lane which housed Suraj Bharadwaj's family. Suraj liked and fell in love with the soft spoken Shobha when he was a teenager. He did not declare his love for Sobha but kept it a secret. He always thought that he would seek Sobha's hand in marriage once he grew up and he had settled down with a good job. But faith had other plans. Sobha's parents fixed her marriage with another boy. Suraj was searching for a job having completed his post graduation. Suraj was beside himself when he heard of Sobha's marriage. A teary eyed Suraj confessed his love in front of his father. He sought his father's help to stop the marriage from happening. Suraj's father tried to convince Sobha's father to postpone the marriage as his son was in love with Sobha. He also proposed Sobha's marriage with his son once Suraj got a job. When Sobha's father refused, he begged him on account of his son. Finally Sobha's father agreed and postponed his daughter's marriage. After a period of six months Suraj gets a job as a lecturer in a local college in Varanasi. Two months later Suraj and Sobha got married with the blessings of the elders.

Suraj Bharadwaj had brought up his children to be good human beings but filled them up with ambitions which the children found it difficult to realize. Each of the children had become a bundle of ambition. Suraj Bharadwaj without ever assessing the capacities of his children pushed them towards achieving things which were unattainable for them. He wanted his children to go to the heights which he himself was unable to reach; putting immense pressure on them to reach the goals defined by him. His family had become a point of coming together of conflicting emotions and high flying ambitions. All seemed to be quite sweet and good for this family from without. However, there was little unanimity that defined the family; it was a family bound together by a flurry of excessive need to stay together to move towards their goals. Sanya was not fully aware of the lack of uniform bonding in the family but she always felt a lack of something in the family. She found it difficult to put a finger to it. She failed to feel the warmth that she needed to make her a secure and happy individual. She suffered from bouts of insecurity which was to plague her for the rest of her life. Sanya always felt the need for someone who will make her feel loved and very secure. She always felt the need for a homely environment.

CHAPTER 3

Arshan Wadia is a strikingly handsome man; handsome enough to own the "cliche" of sweeping a woman off her feet every time he set eyes on one of the fairer sex. Many a woman had fallen for this Adonis like man and some of them had even had their hearts broken by him. Arshan was swayed by the beauty of these women but he was not the one to fall in love with them. The language of love did not influence him in a way it influenced a youthful mind. Arshan was not very enamored with being taken up by the idea of love.

The Wadias lived in their ancestral home in Mumbai. Arshan grew up with his parents and grandparents in this very house. He had done his schooling in Mumbai and had gone to America to complete his masters in Business Administration. Arshan's father, Adel Wadia, inherited the company from his father. Two generations before him had run the family owned steel company. The company was started with hundred workers, two managers and one engineer. Over the years it grew slowly until it was turned into a multimillion dollar company by Adel Wadia. Under Adel's able leadership and his vision, the company flourished and acquired a name and status in the Indian scheme of things. Adel Wadia was an ambitious but upright man. He wanted his company to grow big but not at the cost of the ethics he held on to. He always maintained cleanliness in his business dealings. He was happy that way. He was helped in his endeavours by close friend, Jehangir Irani, whom he had invited to join in the company. In due course of time Adel made Jehangir one of the directors in the company. Jehangir was his friend and slowly became his most trusted confidante. Adel would discuss with Jehangir all the strategies and policies which he wanted to undertake for his company before placing it before the Board of Directors.

At the age of thirty, Adel married a beautiful Parsi girl named Tanaz. It was an arranged marriage. The match was made by one of Adel's aunts. Tanaz was ten years younger to her husband. She belonged to a wealthy family of Mumbai. After two years of her marriage to Adel Wadia she gave birth to a son. They name the boy Arshan. Tanaz was at a loss after her marriage to Adel Wadia. She expected romantic overtures from her husband. She was herself a very romantic person. Her hopes were however dashed as Adel turned out to be a not so romantic person. For Adel, marriage meant responsibility towards his partner and the making of a stable family. He tried his best to provide all the accoutrements that he thought would be needed by his wife but all this involved no feelings of love. Tanaz was greatly distressed by this lack of love in her marriage. She felt in a way trapped and to release this feeling Tanaz, after the birth of Arshan, would spend most of her time away from her home. She travelled abroad and would spend her days in some European country. Sometimes she would take Arshan with her and sometimes she left him in the care of her mother in law, Parinaaz Wadia. Arshan as he grew up found love and comfort in the company of his grandmother. His grandmother became his childhood ally. Arshan found his mother rather aloof and in some world of her own. This prevented him from forming a close bond with his mother. But he loved her anyway. He looked upon his father with love and admiration. When he was growing up he looked upon his father as this colossus who ruled the world. He almost idolized his father. He would happily go with his father whenever Adel took him to the Company office or to the factory. He looked on wide eyed as his father gave directions to his subordinates and enjoyed the whole process.

While he was in the United States of America, Arshan's father suffered a stroke and had to be hospitalized. Arshan had to return to Mumbai and take over the reins of the company for a short amount of time till his father recovered. His short stay in Mumbai during this time made Arshan aware of the course he wanted the company to trace. He wanted the company mired in traditional ways to transform into a more dynamic and modern company. He wanted the steel company to diversify into many different fields. Arshan took steps in the direction of turning the company into a company with modern ways of thinking and modern methodology of working. In this small time, Arshan Wadia succeeded in infusing dynamism and modernism into the company.

Arshan's days in America were blissful days. He loved the independent, anonymous life he led there. He loved the campus life at the college he studied in. He loved the way his professors approached the subjects in the course with deftness and with a skill which would bring forth the innovative instincts of a student. The students did not just attend the lectures in college as a one way transaction but took active part in their classes. Arshan hired two rooms in the first floor of a house which was about one mile from the college. Arshan had hired the rooms from its owner who was an elderly lady and who herself lived on the ground floor with her sister. The arrangement was that the owner would provide him with breakfast and with dinner. Everyday Arshan would eat his breakfast with the two sisters. Breakfast would include sandwiches, eggs, sausages and pancakes. He would also have dinner with them which consisted of mostly a chicken dish, salad, bread and rice. During these sittings with the two sisters the conversation was limited and the sisters talked mostly about things that concerned them so that Arshan always felt like an outsider. He always felt left out. The truth was that Arshan too was not much interested in making himself available for conversation. He was happy to eat in silence. In the second year of college Arshan got involved with a girl named Carla Williams. Carla Williams was two years older than Arshan. She was completing her PhD in Economics. Carla was a lovely girl with long black hair covering her head and with long legs. She would walk with her head bent and looked like a model walking the ramp. Arshan met her while looking up for books at the college library. Carla and Arshan got talking about their studies. One month after coming to know each other Carla and Arshan started their relationship. They started dating each other. They made a beautiful couple- Tall, Handsome and Beautiful. Carla shared an apartment with her college mate, Laila. She and Arshan would often travel for their classes to college together. During recess the couple would have their lunch together. They would sit in the shade of the trees that grew in the college campus. They would hold hands and kiss. Their relationship continued till Arshan completed his degree and returned to India. Both of them promised each other to keep in touch.

Arshan's father was much pleased with the way his young son had veered the company in his absence; so that when Arshan finally completed his studies and came back to India, he handed over the control of the company to Arshan and thereby retired from active life. Arshan took over the company from his father and started the long innings of running the company till his retirement. As Arshan took charge of the company's affairs he seeped deeper and deeper into the business world. Arshan and Carla kept in touch with each other after Arshan's departure from America. Carla especially wrote to Arshan regularly. At first Arshan would reply to her letters with some regularity. But the regularity slowly ceased as Arshan became more and more busy with his work. Arshan tried to make up for his irregularity in replying to Carla's letters by himself writing long emails to her when he could find the time. Arshan even wrote to Carla that he would very much like if she would visit him in India. Carla at the beginning of their association did not know that Arshan belonged to such a rich family. To Carla, Arshan always came across as a simple boy for Arshan did not display any of the indulgences of wealthy boys. She was surprised when Arshan told her that his father owned a company which he is likely to take over when his father retired. The emails and the phone calls which were the only means of communication between the couple became fewer as days went by. The couple did not end their affair formally but as their communication with each other ended so did their affair.

Arshan started to live on his own after assuming charge of the family business. He bought an impressive mansion in Mumbai with sprawling lawns surrounding it. It was a two storied building and modern architecture defined it. It was a square building built to suit the modern décor that lay inside of its being. The spacious living room and the kitchen occupied much of the space on the first floor. A small room in one corner of the first floor housed the cupboards in which the many kinds of firearms belonging to Arshan found their place. Arshan was an avid lover of guns and was himself a good shooter. Arshan practices every day early in the morning at the shooting range that he had built in one end of the huge acres of land that surrounded his mansion. Arshan had learnt to shoot when he held friend Victor's grandfather's rifle for the first time at the age of fourteen. It was the old man, Victor's grandfather, who taught the two young men, Arshan and Victor to fire and shoot with alertness and finesse. This was in Sweden where Arshan was holidaying with his parents and was staying in Victor's father's home for a few weeks. The tricks with the rifle that Arshan carried away with him from Sweden stayed with him and shooting became a hobby with him. It gave a feeling of being powerful and wholesome.

Arshan recalled his days spent with Victor in Sweden with a sense of thrill. Victor's family resided in the northern part of Sweden in a town called Kiruna. A large part of northern Sweden is covered by forests. The men of the two families would wander out to the less thicker parts of the forests for adventure seeking and to feel one with the natural elements there. Arshan's father especially sought out this place of all the places in Europe so as to experience some peace and tranquility away from his work heavy life in India. The women in the families stayed back home, prepared savoury dishes and generally relaxed when the men were gone. Arshan and Victor with guns in their hands went in search of rabbits which if they found them they would shoot with their guns. They manage to kill a couple of rabbits. Both are happy that they could now boast of their prowess with the gun in front of their friends. While in the search for rabbits, Victor and Arshan discover a cave like house hidden from the eye by a group of trees surrounding it. The low branches of the trees fell on the ceiling of the roof giving one the impression that the branches were growing outward from the roof itself. To the two youngsters the house seemed as one straight out of a fairytale. They see one wooden door in the front of the house but it is shut. Both of them go near to the house and find that a side window is open. They peep through the window and see a bearded man bent over a stove cooking something. As they look inside, the man sees them and shouts out to them. Both Victor and Arshan walk away. In the next instant they find the man running towards them waving an axe with his hand. The two of them run for fear of being caught by the man. They run so fast that they outrun the man soon but in their attempt to get away from the man they take the wrong path and get lost in the forest. They are desperate to find their way back home as night was coming soon and it could turn out to be dangerous to stay in the open forest at night. Both of them try to remember the way back but in vain. As they are contemplating what they should do, they could hear the voices of their fathers calling out for them. Obviously the party finding their sons missing for a long time had come searching for them. As the group reunite, rain start to fall. All of them get on to the jeep and drive back to the town. The remembrance of this incident always brought a smile to Arshan's face.

The second floor of the building consisted of an altogether six rooms including the master bedroom, two other bedrooms and three other smaller rooms. An all encompassing balcony covered the second floor on the inside just outside the rooms. A common balcony also lay on the outer side of the rooms. A flight of stairs led from the first floor into the balcony on the second floor and then into the individual rooms on this floor. Every room on the second floor opened up into the outer balcony and the balcony in turn would open up into the swimming pool situated down below on the ground. A group of trees surrounded the swimming pool. The living room on the first floor was surrounded by a balcony on the outside which overlooked the swimming pool. One could open the back door of the living room, reach the balcony and climb down a few steps to reach the garden below with the swimming pool in it. The sprawling lawns which the mansion was bounded with was filled with trees and manicured gardens with a variety of flowers in them. A bevy of private security guards kept close watch on the mansion at all times.

The living room was tastefully decorated with two sets of leather sofas, china vases, chandeliers and a host of vases with fresh flowers adorned the intricately carved tables placed on the four corners of the living room. Paintings costing a fortune hung on the walls of the living room. A small bar was situated on one corner of the living room. It was here in this mansion that Arshan Wadia hosted small, intimate parties for his family and close friends. There was however an exception to this. It was almost a rule with Arshan that he never invited his girlfriends over to his house. He held them as a species to be held afar from his heart and hearth.

CHAPTER 4

Arshan Wadia had inherited the perfect genes of his parents. He possessed strikingly handsome features. A square face, a beautifully pointed nose, deep set eyes and sensuous mouth defined the features of his face. His gait and his manners added to his charm. He walked with a slight forward tilt of his head. He was a tall man almost nearing six feet. The manner in which he talked to just anyone, old or young, with an engaging smile and with eyes sparkling with interest made one and all feel special, leaving them feeling happy. They would feel that he put all his interest in them only. Arshan did not put up a show of oneness with all he talked to. He did pay interest and listened with genuine interest and concern. It was a feeling amongst all classes of people who came in touch with Arshan that this man who hailed from such a distinguished and wealthy family possessed such a sweet manner so as to treat all with the same equanimity. This quality of Arshan fascinated and delighted a lot of people.

Arshan had a sense of being attractive to women since his teenage days. The thought crossed his mind during his high school days when he started to get flowers, candies from the girls in the school. Some girls would be quite open about the fact that they were attracted to him. Some would stealthily convey to him about their liking for him either through a sweet smile or a quaint look at him. He did not accept nor did he return the gestures. One day his eyes fell upon a girl in his school; a lovely girl who studied in the same class as his but in a different section. The students in a class were divided into three sections of thirty students each. Each section would sit in different rooms. The whole school would come together during the morning assembly. Arshan would always look out for the girl and on seeing her his heart would leap up. He, however, could not make up his mind to express his liking for her. He was afraid that she might not like it and reject him. It would be a jolt to his pride. He was scared that his friends would make fun of him if he failed to woo the girl. Arshan takes courage and makes his move and expresses his feelings to Nidhi. Nidhi is the name of the girl with whom Arshan was taken up for some time now. On hearing him speak, Nidhi lightly smiles at him and walks away without saying a word leaving Arshan disappointed and confused. After a time of two days Nidhi walks up to Arshan and expresses her acceptance of his proposal of love. Arshan is joyous at this flowering of his nascent love.

Arshan's relationship with Nidhi was anything but lovely. It was the budding of first love. It was innocent and naive. It was a mix of admiration and a feeling of pride for your loved one. It was a time when everything seemed so light and so easy. Every emotion seemed to flow so effortlessly without any hindrance and without the complexities of the world. Arshan and Nidhi would exchange furtive glances at each other when in the presence of their teachers. When they were away from their teacher's presence they would sit on the stairs of their school building and utter sweet things to each other. They would sometimes hold hands secretly and enjoy the warmth of their touch. Arshan and Nidhi were together for two years and as the two years were coming to an end, Nidhi's father was transferred to Pune. Nidhi had to leave the school and accompany her family to Pune. The two young lovers had a painful separation. They made promises to each other to keep in touch with each other. Arshan was in pain and remained so for sometime. In the initial days of the separation, he frequently wrote fervent messages to his beloved espousing eternal love for her. When he got an answer from Nidhi, Arshan would be overjoyed. He would regularly watch his phone for any message from Nidhi. The two of them kept in touch with each other through the months. But slowly time and distance had its effect on the relationship. Arshan became busy with his studies and his friends. The messages he sent to Nidhi slowly became few in number. He slowly and without being much aware himself started to lose interest in Nidhi. His responses to her messages became short and far in between. After some months, Arshan had all but forgotten about her. Nidhi ceased to exist in his life.

Arshan pass out of school and join college. In college too, he finds himself surrounded by a similar environment of admiration and all round attention from the female folks. Arshan as he goes through college gains more subtlety in the handling of his female counterparts. He now walks in and out of these relationships with ease and with a deft handling of each of these relationships. He now hardly has any emotional connection with these women. He feels women adds beauty to one's life and make life more livable. Arshan felt that women provided a necessary distraction to life's incongruities. They were also much fun to have around. Some of the women flirted with him and they wanted to have a good time with him. Arshan's wealthy lifestyle was a great attraction as he could give them a taste of the good life by giving them rides in his fast cars, luxury yacht and by giving treats in the fancy restaurants. He knew how to keep these women happy. He could almost read the minds of these women. Arshan, however, never allowed himself in any way to be involved emotionally with any of these women. He remained aloof and always thought that a feeling of love; that very emotion would hinder the very thing he held dear – the freedom to live a free life. Whenever he felt that a relationship was becoming an encumbrance and was impeding his life, Arshan immediately drew a line and conveyed to the woman that he could give her so much and no more. He would also abruptly break off a relationship without even an explanation if he felt that it was pulling him into a web of emotions where he had to expend too much of himself.

Arshan's relationship with Sheetal was a good one. Sheetal was good looking, intelligent and possessed an attractive personality. Arshan loved to spend time with her. Sheetal gave him the space to be his own person. She was not clingy and she was secure enough not to want his attention all the time. Arshan could do his own thing and also be in a relationship with her. He was happy. She was the only girlfriend of his with whom he had a steady relationship. It was after one year of the relationship that things started to change between them. He found that slowly Sheetal's attitude towards him had changed. She had started to demand to know about his whereabouts which led Arshan to feel that she did not trust him. Once when Arshan was late in coming to meet her, she said," Where have you been? I need to know where you were." Finding her anxious Arshan tried to assuage her and said," I was with Shekhar. His father was hospitalized. I went to inquire about his health." " You should have told me about it, Sheetal said. Arshan was irritated at these exchange of words but keeps his cool. Then there started to occur a series of incidents in the near future when

Arshan and Sheetal started to have small arguments. Sheetal had started to demand more of Arshan's time. In the beginning of their relationship, Sheetal would be happy if Arshan found out time to meet her. But now she was not satisfied with that. She wanted Arshan to meet her more often. She had started to give him hints that she wanted a long term commitment from him. This alarmed Arshan. He was in no mood for any long term commitment. He told her so without mincing any words. Arshan broke off his relationship with Sheetal leaving her heartbroken and in a lot of pain. After this break up, Arshan continued his foray into the hearts and minds of women. He had a series of relationships with other women and gained the reputation of being a heartbreaker. No one woman could touch his heart emotionally.

CHAPTER 5

Sanya and her father travelled to Mumbai so that Sanya could join in the Tata Institute of Social Sciences so as to begin her internship at the Institute. Sanya settled herself in a hostel room provided by the Institute. Suraj Bharadwaj, after seeing his daughter comfortably settled into her new environment bids his daughter goodbye and leaves for Varanasi.

Sanya was the only occupant in her hostel room for one week before she was joined by another intern named Jennifer Gonsalves. Jennifer belonged to Goa and had come to Mumbai to advance her career. Both the women occupied a square room which was big enough to hold two single beds, two tables and one chair for each table. There were two wall almirahs for each of them. The two women made their best efforts to settle down well in the compact room. On day one, Jennifer unpacked her things and placed her clothes in the almirah and her books she arranged on the table. Sanya watched Jennifer intently. She wondered what her room mate was like and if they would get along well. This she did after exchanging the introductory pleasantries.

Sanya was brought out of her musings by a question put forth by Jennifer. Jennifer asked," Where are you from, Sanya?" "Well, I am from Varanasi," said Sanya. "I have heard of the place. It's a holy place of the people of the Hindu faith," spoke Jennifer. "It definitely is," uttered Sanya. Sanya liked the fact that Jennifer took an interest in Indian culture. Sanya was herself interested in all aspects of Indian as well as western culture and thought she found an apt ally in Jennifer. At least they had something in common to discuss about. This was the beginning of a great friendship between the two women which would stand the test of time. Great friendships are formed in the most likely circumstances in the most unlikely coming together of varied minds.

On the second day of their meeting, Sanya and Jennifer get ready and leave together for their classes in the Institute. Sanya and Jennifer found the premises of the Institute much interesting as also the lectures by the faculty members much engaging. Their minds were freshened up by the new viewpoints presented by the faculty members. They found the faculty members dedicated and full of their own beliefs and perspectives with which they taught their students with much eloquence. These new perspectives to the knowledge the students had already acquired before added new dimensions to their thought process and allowed them to think anew on a lot of ideas that were inculcated in their minds through years of study till now. Sanya had an active mind perhaps leaning a little on the hyperactive side. She found the whole academic atmosphere not only very refreshing but she could attune easily to it and it did excite her a lot. Her mind fully embraced the excitable and intelligent atmosphere which blew about the Institute.

Sanya and Jennifer would have their meals together, do their shopping together, learn some of their lessons together. The two friends were inseparable from the very beginning of their friendship.

The two of them were very different in their approach to their lives –
if Sanya was reserved, Jennifer was an exuberant character. Just like
there were differences in their looks too – Sanya kept her hair long
and loved classic Indian clothes; Jennifer kept her hair short and
mostly wore western clothes. Another habit of Sanya which irritated
Jennifer and she often chided Sanya for it was that Sanya was a little
bit untidy with the arrangement of her books and her clothes.
Jennifer was tidiness personified. Jennifer was punctilious to a fault;
while Sanya was a little bent towards the wilder side of things in that
if she got irritated to an extent, Sanya would lose her cool and could
be blunt with her words and a little bit off with her behaviour. The
two friends were however brought together by a simplistic view
towards life; a life of no great wealth but a life full of love and
liveliness. Both had visions of an all encompassing love which
would hold sway over their lives and be the source of all their
happiness and fulfillment.

The two women had their first brush with the cosmopolitan
culture of the fast moving city of Mumbai when they interacted with
the other students. Students belonging to the different parts of the
country inhabited the campus of the Institute bringing with them the
diverse cultural influences of the varied regions they came from to
this city. The city was a culmination of the goodness and the
eccentricities of the different cultures combined together. This very
characteristic made the people of this city open for the absorption of
various new ideas in their lives. The two women became good
friends with an intern who belonged to the city named Anita Shroff.
Anita Shroff was a lovely, young women always dressed in shorts,
tops and high heels. She was the sort of women who can make all the
men to look up at her and be attracted to her at least momentarily.
She was to say the least very bohemian in nature. She was open

minded and leaned easily to recklessness in most matters. Sanya was most often than not taken aback by Anita's decisions which Anita took without much consideration as to the consequences which her decisions might trigger. Sanya herself was a woman whose every decision was well thought out. She would consider a matter from all angles before taking a decision. Her decisions were never rash. She never ever rushed into a decision. Although Sanya was not very agreeable to Anita's certain decisions, Sanya loved the fact that Anita was helpful. Sanya also found her lovable. Sanya also loved the courage which Anita had to take the decisions that she did even though these decisions might be deemed as being reckless. It was with Anita that Sanya and Jennifer explored the city of Mumbai with all its historical landmarks as also its nightlife. The first time they travelled to the Marine Drive with Anita and another of three male interns, they felt not only a sense of exhilaration but there was also a certain stillness that entered their hearts and minds. All of them had huddled up in Anita's car and was driven to Marine Drive by Anita. They reached as evening was converging into night and stayed at the Drive all night long. When they were hungry they munched the sandwiches and the burgers they had taken along with them.

Of the three male interns who had accompanied the three women to Marine Drive, one was one named Jacob D'Souza. Jacob had been interested in Jennifer for some time now. Jacob like Jennifer was from Goa. He became interested in Jennifer the first time he saw her in class. The interest had only grown when he started talking to Jennifer in class. He however did not get the right opportunity to tell her about his real feelings for her. "Today would be the best day to express to Jennifer my love for her," thought Jacob. Earlier in the day when Jacob came to know that Jennifer would be going with them to Marine Drive, he immediately agreed to go. He wanted to seize this opportunity to have a talk with Jennifer. It was a clear starlit sky this night. It was as if the cool atmosphere was in harmony with the lovers to espouse their love for each other. With his intent clear in his mind, Jacob comes near Jennifer and asks her," Jennifer, can I have a talk with you alone?" "Yes, of course," Jennifer answers with a look of surprise in her eyes. "Friends, please excuse us for some time," Jacob says to the others in their group. Jacob leads Jennifer a few meters away from their group and to a place where the crowd was thin. He turns to Jennifer and says," You and I belong to the same place. We study at the same Institute. Can't we be together? I like you a lot, Jennifer." "Are you talking about dating each other," Jennifer said talking straight to Jacob. "Yes, I am," replied Jacob. "Well, we can give it a try. I like you a lot too, Jacob," Jennifer tells Jacob. Jacob jumps up with joy at Jennifer's words. He takes Jennifer's hands in his own and presses them. The couple returns hand in hand to find their friends looking at them dumfounded. Anita dropped her friends at the hostel in the morning. All six friends fell into deep sleep after taking bath and after having their breakfast. It was a Sunday and all of them had the day to themselves.

It was when Anita suggested that she along with Sanya and Jennifer go off to a nightclub, Sanya got uncomfortable with the idea. She told Anita of her discomfiture but Anita insisted on her going. She told her that it will be fun and Sanya would enjoy it a lot. Sanya goes to the nightclub to keep her friend happy. Once inside the night club, Sanya starts to get uncomfortable in the dimly lit, noisy place. The dance floor is filled with people gyrating to the loud music being played. Anita and Jennifer leave Sanya to join in the dance and shake a leg. Sanya sips fruit juice and sits in the room listlessly. She tries to enjoy the music but finds it too loud and jarring to the ears. A man approaches her and asks her to dance with him. Sanya tells him that she does not know how to dance. When the man keeps on insisting, Sanya gets up from her seat and rushes outside. She waits outside for the rest of the time for her friends to come out. As she waits she decides that nightclubs and dances were not her kind of enjoyment. She banishes them from her itinerary forever. She would rather stay back at home and indulge in more saner and more quieter activities.

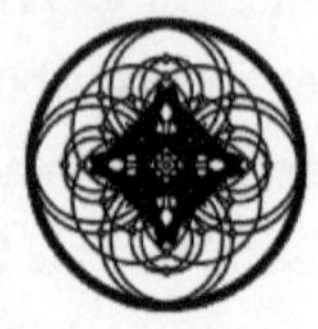

CHAPTER 6

Day transformed into night and night turned to day in the mega city of Mumbai; Sanya breathed in the views and the sensations of this living, thriving city. Although the throb of this city entered Sanya's life and imbued it with new sights and ideas, she was not blown away by the whirlwind into which one could enter in a city like this. Sanya had always been a down to earth girl and could hardly be blown away by any blinding scenario. Sanya did not try to gel in with the people of the city and her singular personality shone through the crowd in the campus at the Institute. She very unconsciously stood out in the student community. Although it was never her intention to do so, it was so. People would notice how beautiful this quiet, pleasant girl was. Sanya would be very much surprised by the attention she garnered from the men folk wherever in her life she seemed to be. Sanya did nothing to catch all the attention; she got it anyway. She was not very pleased with the attentions of the other sex and put up with it with certain amount of scorn. These were not men of her liking and so most of the time she was flustered and irritated.

Sanya was pursued by one of the interns in her class. Ashutosh

Singha was the intern who showed an interest in Sanya ever since their classes first started. He was a tall, gawky fellow with a curious expression on his face. Ashutosh was so smitten with Sanya that he followed her almost everywhere. He would sit beside Sanya in class or if there was no empty seat beside her then he would sit on a seat behind her. He would even at times join Sanya and Jennifer during lunch break and have his lunch with them. He would always join the two women and walk with them till they reached their hostel. Sanya and Jennifer knew of his liking for Sanya though he had not expressed it in so many words. Both the women would get irritated by his facetious remarks and his bad jokes. Sanya was angry with him for making things so obvious to the whole class but out of some basic courtesy she keeps her silence. Ashutosh, when he got to be alone with Sanya expresses to her his love for her. Sanya gets angry with Ashutosh and rebukes him. She tells him that she is not in the least in love with him. She asks him to stay away from her and to leave her alone. Ashutosh tries to reason with her but meets with an angry stare and absolute silence from Sanya.

It was a professor who was her teacher at the Institute who had an eye for Sanya. Professor Aadesh Dwivedi when he started his classes with the new batch of interns was struck by Sanya's beauty. As time went by Sanya revealed a level of intelligence which made him more besotted with her. Sanya could feel the man's attentiveness on her all through the classes he did for them. She would feel embarrassed at so much indulgence that Aadesh would show for her in class. She was thoroughly annoyed with him when his show of utter liking for her became a talking point among the interns in the class. Sanya thought of ending this unnecessary gossip going on among the students. She started to give less and less attention to Aadesh's show of concern for her. Sanya made it clear to him that she was not interested in the advances that he made towards her. She did this without uttering a word but through her show of a certain disdain for the way he had been acting with her. Aadesh did not understand this for a while but when he did get wind of Sanya's dislike for him he stopped acting the way he did. He was also ashamed of his attempts at going all out to please a student of his.

Arshan's cousin sister, Shirin used to give guest lectures at the Tata Institute of Social Sciences. On a Friday on which Shirin was to give a lecture she was down with fever. If she cancelled her lecture at the last minute, the class would be wasted as it would be difficult for the Institute to make any last minute changes. Shirin calls up Arshan and makes a request to him to fill in for her. Arshan after some thought decides to keep his cousin's request.

There is a flutter among the interns in the class as Arshan enters it and is introduced to the interns by a faculty member of the Institute. Arshan starts his lecture and was almost winding up the session when a girl who sat on the second row catches his attention. The girl was none other than Sanya who had let her hair open that day and was busy taking notes. She was wearing a light pink kurta teamed with leggings and was looking serenely beautiful. As Arshan looks at her, Sanya too looks up from her notebook and notices Arshan's gaze on her. Sanya in that momentary glance could see the glint of a smile in Arshan's eyes. Sanya looks at Arshan again out of curiosity and sees him watching her intently. Arshan could see a simple, sweet girl who seemed quite unaware and totally unconcerned about the effect she was having on him. As their eyes met, Sanya looks away and her unconcern for him makes her more desirable to Arshan. Arshan had never encountered a girl looking so unconcernedly away from him. For what was most normal for him was to find women swooning over him. Arshan, in those very first moments that he saw Sanya, felt that he should definitely know the girl more closely. He felt determined to know the girl. So, when the faculty member invited Arshan for lunch, he immediately said that he would have lunch with the interns at the canteen.

The students were pleased to have the opportunity to interact with Arshan on a one on one basis. Sanya was not much taken up with the commotion created by the interns. She took her food from the self serving counter and ate her food quietly at a corner table. Arshan followed Sanya's every movement while he himself had his food. Arshan finishes his food, excuses himself and approaches Sanya. "Excuse me, will you please come out of the canteen. I need to talk to you," Arshan said to Sanya. Sanya, a bit taken aback by Arshan's move uttered, "Ok, sir." So saying, Sanya followed Arshan to the verandah outside of the canteen. Arshan finding Sanya a little nervous asked in a most polite manner, " May I know your name." " Sanya Bharadwaj, sir," answered Sanya in a modest voice. " Where are you from, Sanya?" Arshan asked. " I am from Varanasi. I am doing my internship here," Sanya replied. " Well, I live in Mumbai itself," Arshan told Sanya. "Very well sir," Sanya said. At this Arshan looked at his watch and saw that he was getting late for a meeting. " Sanya, I am getting late for a meeting. I must take your leave now," Arshan said. " Very well sir," Sanya answered. At this, Arshan looked at Sanya giving a searching look at her face as if he was looking for something in that sweet face. He then turns around and walks away. He gets into his car and is driven off leaving Sanya amazed at the preceding events. She could not understand the interest shown by Arshan Wadia towards her. She was a bit puzzled by the look which disconcerted her but which seemed to hold not much meaning in it. Sanya brushes off the thoughts that occupy her mind when Arshan left her alone and proceeds to attend the next class.

In the recess, Sanya related to Jennifer all about the incident with Arshan Wadia. Jennifer too is confounded about the whole matter. Meanwhile the incident had sparked off a series of talking points amongst the students of Sanya's class. Most of them were curious to know what had transpired between Sanya and Arshan. A few of them asked Sanya about it and Sanya told them about the short conversation she had with Arshan Wadia. A lot of the students were convinced that Arshan was interested in Sanya in a romantic way. A few of the girls even grew jealous of Sanya for catching Arshan's eye. Some of the girls set out to save Sanya from Arshan. They told Sanya about Arshan's escapades with other women and how the man was just incapable of being true to one woman. They told her of the many times Arshan had broken a woman's heart. Sanya was a bit bored at all the information fed into her. She thought that she needed no saving from Arshan Wadia as she was in the least interested in him. She had found Arshan strikingly handsome and she quite liked his polite manner towards her but that was all there was to it. The romantic aspect of the whole incident did not in the least bit interested her. It seemed a bit far fetched to her. The wandering thoughts of Arshan Wadia, however, gave Sanya pleasant sensations. Sanya felt good about them but wanted to leave it at that.

Arshan was not sure of the workings of his heart after his chance meeting with Sanya. Sanya seemed to have stirred something primal in him. These primitive feelings were the ones that led to a feeling in Arshan to protect Sanya and to keep her safe under his care. Arshan equated these feelings with love. He admitted to himself that he was in love with Sanya. He was determined to see her again. He wanted to keep her under wraps for himself and shut out the whole outside world from her.

CHAPTER 7

The normalcy of life continued to flow for Arshan and Sanya. Both led their lives as they were supposed to. Only Sanya seemed to seep into Arshan's thoughts whenever he sat back and relaxed a bit in office or she entered his mind when he was resting in bed at night. In such moments Arshan would grow restless and the urge to see Sanya increased. Sanya seemed to coil like a creeper around his thoughts and then he would give in to the physical sensations that would be an aftermath of his thoughts. Sanya was much more relaxed in her situation than Arshan. Though the thoughts of Arshan encumbered her mindspace now and then, yet they were not overpowering enough to make her overcome with emotions for Arshan. Sanya remained calm. The calmness was such that Arshan's thoughts brought her a pleasant thrill to contend with but they did not bring any burning desire to see him. While Arshan was assured of the fact that he wanted to meet Sanya in the near future, such feelings never did arose in Sanya's mind.

The weekend arrives and Arshan decides to throw a party at his house. The only reason he is holding the party is because of his desire to meet Sanya again. Arshan sends a handwritten note to

Sanya and invites her for the party. He also invites some of his close friends over to the party which was to be held on Sunday. Sanya on receiving the note from Arshan is a little surprised. She says to Jennifer," Arshan Wadia has invited me to a party at his house on Sunday." " Oh, that's very exciting," said Jennifer. " But Jennifer, I cannot go alone. I want you to come with me," said Sanya. " But Sanya, he has not invited me to the party," uttered Jennifer. " I know. But I can always ask him if you can accompany me to the party. After all he has given me his phone number. But first you must promise to come with me," Sanya asked of Jennifer. Jennifer, after a bit of cajoling by Sanya, agreed to go to the party with Sanya. Sanya picks up her phone and dials Arshan's phone number. After a few seconds she hears a deep set male voice at the other end of the line. " Hello, this is Sanya Bharadwaj. Good afternoon Mr. Wadia. I wanted to take your permission to bring along my good friend, Jennifer, to the party if you do not have any problems to that," Sanya asked Arshan. " Yes, you can Sanya. Please ask her to come with you. Tell her that I have invited her too," Arshan replied to the soft voice he could hear at the other end. " Thank you. I am so grateful to you," Sanya told Arshan. Saying so, both of them disconnected each other's phone.

Sanya and Jennifer had now to decide on what they would be wearing to the party. Both of them look through their array of clothes and discovered that they had nothing suitable to wear to the party. Both had little knowledge as to the clothes they should wear to a party being hosted by a business tycoon. " Jennifer, we must buy ourselves new dresses to wear to the party. Otherwise we would look very out of place in there," Sanya said. " You are right. Indeed we should buy new clothes and also style our hair in the fashion of the day," opined Jennifer. On Saturday afternoon the women went out shopping. Sanya bought an elaborately embroidered orange coloured salwar suit. Jennifer bought a simple, elegant western gown. Both of them had lunch in a restaurant and then went to a salon to get their hair done. Hair being styled, both women came to their hostel room all flushed with excitement at the thought of the succeeding day's event.

It is Sunday evening; the guests have started arriving in Arshan's house. The guests include Arshan's close friends, company executives and some of his neighbours. Drinks have started to flow and the waiters carried the starters about. The guests partook of the food and the drinks and engaged in small talk. Arshan, dressed in a white shirt and black trousers with a navy blue jacket thrown in was looking dapper and very handsome. If one looked closely one could see that Arshan was not much interested in the guests or the party. Instead his eyes darted often to the front door as if he was anticipating someone's arrival. Of course, he was awaiting Sanya's entry into the party. One hour into the party and Sanya and Jennifer arrives. They are met at the front door by Arshan who had stepped aside from his guests and had come forward to greet them as they came in. " Both of you look stunning," Arshan remarked. " Thank you," Jennifer uttered. Sanya somehow felt tongue tied. She was overcome by the novelty of the occasion. " Please make yourselves comfortable. Will you take some wine?" Arshan asked. " No, we do not drink," said Jennifer. " Then please take some soft drinks," said Arshan. " Thanks Mr Wadia," uttered Jennifer. Arshan finding Sanya very quiet looked at her with curious eyes. " What is it Sanya. Is anything bothering you?" Arshan asked. At this question, Sanya answered," Nothing at all. I am all right."

The night came on and the guests had a buffet dinner which consisted of a combination of Indian and Chinese dishes. Food was delicious and Sanya and Jennifer enjoyed the food thoroughly. After dinner, Arshan could see that Sanya was making her way out into the garden. Arshan on an instinct follows her to the garden. He finds her standing in the moonlight looking out into the garden with the many blooms in it. He goes and stands beside Sanya. Sanya is startled by the noise and looks around. She finds Arshan standing beside her. She smiles up at him and says," You have such a beautiful garden." " Do you like it?" Arshan asks. Sanya nods her head in reply. " Are you always so quiet or is it because you are in a new place?" Arshan asked of Sanya. " I always talk a little less," Sanya answered. Sanya and Arshan look at each other and for a long time they are in communion with each other. They feel drawn to each other. The spell is broken when Jennifer comes out and reminds Sanya that they must leave for their hostel. Arshan arranges for his car to drop them at their hostel. Sanya feels an unexplainable pain to take leave of Arshan. In the few moments that they were alone together, Sanya felt so comfortable in Arshan's presence that now on having to leave him she felt as if she was being ushered away from a home she had known for years. A home that gave her protection and kept her safe. Arshan too felt an union with Sanya. Sanya had somehow lightly brushed across his heart and certainly seemed to hold fast to his heart.

CHAPTER 8

Sanya gets up in the morning feeling a little tired. She and Jennifer had talked late into the night after coming back from the party and had gone to sleep quite late. Both the women in their excitement had so much to talk about that they sat on their beds and talked about it without waiting for the morning to arrive. Sanya is feeling as if she had a hangover of some sort. She freshens up and picks up her phone and suddenly her eyes fall on a message sent by Arshan. Sanya's mood lifts up on seeing the message. Arshan had written," You looked so beautiful yesterday. Thanks for coming to the party. You made my day. Since yesterday I have started to feel very close to you." Arshan had written the message while going to do his exercises at his gymnasium. Arshan would get up very early in the morning and go for shooting practice at the shooting range in the many acres of land surrounding his mansion. He would then go for his regular exercises at the gymnasium.

Sanya was not feeling very clear in her head and as such did not try to read too much into the message from Arshan. She put it off to a later time to decipher any meaning in the letter if there was any meaning in it at all. Sanya was getting late for her classes. She gets ready and together with Jennifer goes off to attend her classes.

Sanya is trying to relax in her room in the hostel after her classes are over, when her phone rings. She looks at it and could see Arshan's name flashing on the screen. She immediately picks it up. " Hello Sanya. I just called to see if you are well," Arshan said. " I am fine. Thanks so much for inviting me to the party. I enjoyed very much," Sanya replied. Arshan went on to say," Sanya, I am happy you enjoyed yourself. I called to invite you to my home and have lunch with me tomorrow. This time I want you to come alone. Since you are now familiar with me and my house, I think you will be comfortable to come on your own. I would like to talk to you alone." Sanya was silent for a time and then spoke," I will come." " I am happy you have agreed to come and see me," Arshan said to Sanya. Today Sanya went to bed early as she wanted to feel fresh and be in a good mood the next morning. She wanted to give all her attention to Arshan when she is at his side during lunch the next day. Arshan was on a high when he went to bed and fell asleep. The thought of meeting Sanya the next day triggered happy thoughts in his mind and sleep came early.

Sanya gets dressed in a white sari with red roses printed on it. She wears matching earrings and the gold bangles that she wore every day. Sanya feels calm today when she thinks about the impending luncheon with Arshan. She does not feel any of the excitement that she felt when she attended his party. This transformation of feelings is due to the familiarity that she and Arshan had struck since their second meeting at the party and the easy friendship that was born out of this familiarity. Sanya arrives in Arshan's house for lunch and is welcomed by him. Both are instantly happy to see each other and both find their hearts racing. They sit down in the living room and partake of the fruit juice and the starters.

Arshan asked Sanya," You told me that your family is from Varanasi. Who all are there in your family?" " Well, my family consists of my parents, my younger sister and my brother. I am the eldest," Sanya said. " Who all constitutes your family?" Sanya asked Arshan. Arshan stated," I am the only child of my parents. My parents live in Mumbai but in our ancestral home. My grandmother too stays with them."

Sanya looks around the living room and admires the paintings. She says," I like paintings although I do not have much of paintings. I especially like landscapes." Sanya added," Can I have a look at your garden outside? Last time I saw it only during night time." " Yes, of course," Arshan replied. Arshan led Sanya into the garden outside. Sanya looked around the garden as the two of them walked about. She especially loved the flowers and pointing to the rose plants in full bloom in the garden she remarked all of a sudden," I love roses." " Well, I must tell the gardener to plant more roses," said Arshan. Arshan made this remark spontaneously without much of a thought. Sanya looks up at Arshan and smiles a slow smile. Arshan too responds with a smile. Both had no idea as to why Arshan said that thing about growing more roses. But both looked at the other and when their eyes met there was perfect understanding of a growing attraction and closeness between Sanya and Arshan. Pointing to a bench in the garden, Arshan said," Sanya, let us sit in that bench." Sanya obliges and both of them sit in the bench. Arshan says," Sanya, I must tell you that I like you a lot. I sense a feeling of togetherness whenever I meet you or even think about you. I want whatever we have at present to continue. I want you to be with me." Hearing this Sanya tells Arshan," I too feel very close to you when I am with you. I feel very safe with you. But you must give me time to sort out my own feelings." " Let us stay with each other till we are sure of our feelings for each other," Arshan said. Sanya looked at him and nodded her head in agreement. The two of them come into the house and have lunch over some lively conversation. Sanya and Arshan chattered on for quite sometime as if there was no care in the world. They go their separate ways after having lunch.

CHAPTER 9

Two weeks after their luncheon, it was imperative for Arshan to leave for the United Kingdom for finalizing the takeover of the British Steel Company. During his stay Arshan would be based in London. He would have to initially stay in London for at least three months. First, there was the task of finalizing the bid for the takeover of the company and then to restructure the British company and bring it to conform to his own terms and conditions. He would have to strive for the inclusion of the company under the aegis of the Indian company he runs. He would have to look into the workings of the company and the workforce. Arshan would have to see if the manpower required any modernizing and refurbishing. With these tasks in hand, Arshan Wadia was to leave Mumbai for London. A bunch of his company's executives would accompany him so as to help him in rebuilding the British Company.

As Arshan prepares to leave for London, his first thoughts fall upon Sanya. Immediately he could visualize Sanya's visage. Arshan becomes restless as his heart stirs with the thoughts of Sanya. He knows he must set up a meeting with her and assure her. Arshan again invites Sanya to his house on a Friday evening before his departure on the evening of Saturday. Sanya, as she meets Arshan and sets her eyes on him, breaks into a smile. The smile conveys to Arshan clearly as to how happy Sanya is to see him. A pain starts in Arshan's heart. He is dismayed at having to sadden the one person who for some weeks now meant all to him.

Arshan takes Sanya outside to the garden and both of them sit down in the same bench they sat on an earlier day. Arshan looks at Sanya and addresses her with a sad smile on his face," Sanya, I have to go to London on a business trip. I would be away from Mumbai for at least three months. I am to finalize the takeover of a British Company. I called you out here today to bid you goodbye." Sanya looks at Arshan with startled eyes but she says nothing. She keeps her head bent and do not look up at Arshan. Arshan leans towards Sanya and with his hands takes one of Sanya's hand in his own and places it on his chest. Sanya slowly look up at him with pain in her eyes. She felt at that moment that something precious was being taken away from her. At that moment she felt as if she had known Arshan for long years. As he placed Sanya's hand on his chest Arshan said," You reside here; in my heart." Sanya raises her eyes to Arshan's and smiles. Arshan could clearly see the glint of tears in her eyes. " I am coming back to you Sanya. There is nothing to worry about," Arshan assures Sanya. He bends forward and kisses Sanya's forehead. These moments of togetherness made love flow amongst the couple though "love" as a word has not been admitted into their world.

Saturday arrives and Arshan boards the plane for London. As he sat on his seat he clearly remembers the words of Sanya," I will wait for your return," which Sanya had said the day before. He closes his eyes in remembrance. Sanya is in her hostel room feeling a sense of emptiness which she had never recognized before.

CHAPTER 10

Arshan lands in London and is swept into a whirlpool of activities giving him little time to think about himself or the things which were close to him. He was immediately involved in hectic negotiations for bringing the control of the British company to his own control. Preliminary negotiations were over, being done by the other executives of the two companies. The final negotiations were done with Arshan heading the Indian side of the team. After two weeks of hard negotiations, the final modalities for the takeover of the British Company were worked out and finally the takeover of the British Steel Company took effect. The process if it excited and satisfied Arshan, also tired him a lot.

In the weeks leading to the taking over of the reins of the British Steel Company, Arshan had little time to spare for his family and for Sanya. When he first landed in London, Arshan said perfunctory greetings to his family and to Sanya. He thought that the people close to him would understand his absolute lack of time for them. His parents were used to their son being busy with his work and so made no complaints. But Sanya was not in the habit of knowing Arshan's work routine; nor did she know that his work occupied most of his time. For Arshan, it was like nurturing the company like one brings up a baby as he tried to strengthen his company. Sanya, unaware of all this, started to have misgivings about Arshan. She longed to talk and communicate with Arshan for longer time. She wanted his attention. Sanya thought that even if there was much distance between them now, there should be better communication between the two of them. Sanya in recent times had started to worry about her relationship with Arshan even as she became sure about what her heart wanted. A sudden spark was lighted while she was away from Arshan and she wanted to give vent to her feelings so much that she was singed on the inside. Sanya just wanted Arshan to be near to her.

Meanwhile it was almost two months since Arshan's departure from Mumbai. Sanya was on the verge of finishing her internship. She and Jennifer actively searched for jobs in Mumbai. Both had decided to stay on in Mumbai. Both of them felt that the city held immense potential for growth of an individual both on a personal level as well as on the career front. Sanya and Jennifer both landed jobs in the private sector just as they were finishing their internship. Both were joyous with their achievements. Both the friends decided to stay together after their internship was over. Sanya and Jennifer searched for an affordable apartment to stay in after they would have to vacate their hostel room. They came upon a suitable apartment which was to their liking. It consisted of a small living room, two small bedrooms, and a kitchen. It was situated on the second floor. It had the added advantage of a good sized balcony. The two women went shopping on a weekend and bought the minimal furniture including two single beds, a pair of table and chair for each of them. They bought a sofa set for the living room and a few paintings to decorate the room with. They bought some flower pots and placed them in the balcony and planned to plant flowers in the near future. They also bought the utensils and crockery they would require for the kitchen. On Sunday, both women left their hostel and started living in the apartment they had taken on rent.

Sanya was happy to have been successful in so far that she had completed her internship well and had immediately got a job without much of a lay off. She had earlier talked to her father about her decision to stay on in Mumbai after she finished her internship. She also informed him of her decision to take up a job in Mumbai and thus start a career in the city. Though her father was a bit apprehensive about Sanya's decision to reside in Mumbai alone but his fears were laid to rest when he found that Sanya had a new confidence about her after spending all those months at the Institute. Suraj Bharadwaj was also not very happy to let his eldest daughter stay away from him and he hesitantly agreed to Sanya's appeal and her decision.

It is true that a new courage and confidence had taken the place of the initial diffidence that Sanya suffered from when she first arrived in Mumbai. If charting out a career was one of the reasons Sanya had for staying on in Mumbai, she also wanted to be close to Arshan. Mumbai also happened to be the city where the man who had aroused love in her being stayed. It was Arshan Wadia's hometown. This very fact would not allow Sanya to leave this place which now seems hallowed to Sanya. Everything attached to Arshan seems to be likeable to Sanya and in a way touched with magic and completion.

CHAPTER 11

Sanya joins a multinational company as a financial analyst. She is excited and happy at the prospect of earning a living and being on her own. She gets herself new sets of clothes keeping up with the fashion trends of the day. She looks radiant on her first day at office dressed in a plain white shirt and black trousers with white strips on it. She reaches office as the office peon is opening the locks to the office door. She asks him about the office manager, Animesh Biswas. The peon replies that he would be arriving soon. Sanya was the first person to reach office. In her anxiety to reach office on time, she had reached the office half an hour before the start of office time which was at ten o'clock. She had to wait outside for a while as the cleaner swept and swabbed the office floor and cleaned the desks. When the cleaning gets over, the peon calls her in and asks her to sit in the waiting room. Sanya sits down and take a deep breath. She was getting anxious by the minute as to what was coming up for her. The initial euphoria she had felt was slowly petering out. As she sat waiting for the manager to arrive, one male and two female employees come in and take their place in the office. They look at her with curious glances and in low voices inquire of the peon as to who she was. There is a steady flow of employees into the office but there is no sign of the arrival of the manager. After some time the peon comes to the waiting area and tells Sanya that the manager would like to see her.

Sanya enters the manager's chamber and finds him standing at his desk rummaging through some papers. Animesh Biswas is a man of average height, round faced and slightly bald. He was well into his forties. Sanya greets him. Animesh Biswas indicates to a chair in front of his desk and asks Sanya to sit down. Sanya sits in the chair. He asks Sanya about the things she is adept in as far as financial matters were concerned. Sanya spells out the things she is comfortable with. He tells Sanya that she would have to get some training and assigns her under another financial analyst, Naina Rai. He would himself give Sanya certain tasks from time to time which Sanya would have to execute. Animesh asks the peon to call Naina to his chamber. As Naina comes in, she gives a quick glance at Sanya. Animesh introduces Sanya to Naina. " Sanya will be under your care for some time till she picks up the skills properly," Animesh addressed Naina. " Alright, sir, Naina said.

Sanya starts her work in the company. She sits in a cubicle and diligently tries to complete her work given to her by Naina and sometimes by the manager. Naina keeps a keen eye on Sanya's progress. Naina is a tall, small built girl with an oval face. Sanya found her knowledgeable but not very bright nor very intelligent. The thing that became a thorn between the two women was the growing dislike of Naina of the speed with which Sanya mastered the subjects that were given to her by Naina. It made Naina insecure to an extent that Naina started to talk down to Sanya. This became very irritable to Sanya. Sanya was relieved when after a couple of months Animesh felt that Sanya has had enough of training and started to give her independent work to do.

Jennifer and Jacob worked in the same company. Both of them appeared in an interview in a company and were absorbed in the company. They travelled to work together. Jacob lived in a lane quite close to Jennifer's apartment. He had bought a bike with some portion of his first salary. He would drive to Jennifer's apartment, pick her up and then both of them would drive off to work. The couple had a gala time together. They spent most of their time together. They would even travel to their home state of Goa together. The two lovers came so close to each other that they decided to spend their lifetime together. Having been in a comfortable position in their lives for quite sometime now, they decided to inform their families of their decision to marry one another. Jennifer informed Sanya of their decision. Sanya is happy for the couple. Her heart, however, wrenched from the pain she felt when she saw Jacob and Jennifer together as it reminded her of Arshan and her separation from him. The pain was bad then. It was as bad as it could get. Sanya masked her pain well so that it was not visible even to her best friend. The foursome, Sanya, Anita, Jennifer and Jacob would spend most of their free time hanging out in Marine Drive having roasted corn and tea. Sanya often wondered with a sigh," Only if Arshan could be here beside me. It would have been perfect."

Anita joined and started working with an international Non Governmental Organisation. It was Anita's idea to combine her service life with a bit of charity work. She thought that working with an NGO would provide her this perfect opportunity. As such she joined it and delved whole heartedly into her work. The NGO worked for the mental and physical well being of women and children. Anita chose to work with the women who were at a disadvantage due to their economic or their physical circumstances.

At first Anita used to get shocked at the immense hardships some of these women faced as also angry at the atrocities some of these women had to face. The initial shock however made her resolve more strong to be of some help to these women. Anita sincerely wanted to uplift these women from the despicable conditions they lived in. She would sometimes feel depressed and helpless on seeing these women. Like the anger which overcame her when she met this teenage girl who was rendered pregnant by her lascivious teacher. But due thought to the situation made her realize that the solution to all these ills lay not in anger but in channelling this anger to bring the culprits to justice and helping the victim to cope with life and lead them to a life filled with hope and economic self sufficiency.

CHAPTER 12

Arshan lived in a house owned by his family in London. He would regularly do his running in the early morning. After bath and breakfast, Arshan would let himself be driven to the premises of the British company which had come under his control. He would everyday sit down at his chair and study the structure of the company. He would have to decide as to where he was to start to restructure the company. He finally decided to start working from the bottom to the top of the company. Arshan wanted a definite change in the structure of the company and he was determined to make the change a reality. He diligently worked towards this end. Arshan would be worn out as the evening arrived. He would get home and relax with some music. He would sometimes pour himself a drink. As the night came on, so also sleep would arrive and take him in its arms very conveniently. Arshan led a very regular life during these two months.

Arshan gets up one morning and looks at his phone. He is surprised to see a message from Sanya. It simply read," When are you coming back?" Arshan could very well understand the tone that underlay the message. He at once knew that Sanya was missing him and he instinctively knew that Sanya wanted to be with him. Arshan instantly decides to leave for India. He informs his office that he would be unavailable for the next three days as he would travel to India. Arshan wanted to meet Sanya and express his love for her. He could sense that Sanya too was in love with him and wanted to say things to him that he now knew that he was eagerly waiting all this while to hear from her. Arshan had a heightened sense of intuition about the state of mind of his beloved.

Arshan arrives in India on Sunday afternoon. He goes straight to his home where he takes a light lunch and gets some sleep. In the evening he gets ready to meet Sanya. He had looked forward to this meeting since he received Sanya's message. He was excited about this meeting since he boarded the flight back to India. Sanya is alone in the house when Arshan knocks at the door. Jennifer had gone home for the weekend. Sanya opens the door and Arshan steps in. Sanya is startled to see him as Arshan had come unannounced to her house. She utters his name," Arshan," and runs into his arms. Sanya hold Arshan tight against her. " My love," Arshan says and lifts Sanya in his arms and carries her to the bedroom and puts her down in her bed. Arshan then lies down beside Sanya and kisses her deeply on the lips. He then kisses her cheeks, her chin, her neck. Sanya cries out," I love you. I love you a lot." " I love you too, Sanya," Arshan says. Arshan slowly gets up and sits up in the bed beside Sanya. Sanya too sits up with her back propped up against the headboard of the bed. Arshan says to Sanya," My only purpose of coming to India is to meet you. I missed you a lot while in London. I might have been far away but my thoughts have always been with you, dear." " I felt lost without you these couple of months. Time seems to pass off so slowly when you absolutely want to see the one you love," Sanya says to Arshan. She again states," I cannot tell you how happy I am to see you again." The two lovers talked on for a long time into the night.

In Goa, Jacob and Jennifer spend the day in a sombre mood with nervous energy flowing through their beings. This is the day when their parents would meet. The two families would meet at a seaside restaurant in the evening and have dinner together. Jennifer and Jacob had made the reservation at the restaurant for thirty people. Their parents would be joined by a number of relatives and friends on both sides. When Jennifer and Jacob had pronounced their love for each other in front of each of their parents, their parents had wanted to meet with each of them and their families. The couple then set up the meeting in the restaurant. The day rolls into the evening. The evening comes with the dying rays of the sun painting the western sky with a reddish hue. The Goan people and its culture are colourful and joyous. Their culture is engaging and energizing. Merry crowds gather at the restaurant making merry having glasses of wine and delicious seafood. The couple await the arrival of their families. The two families arrive and take their places at the restaurant. For the relief of the two lovers there was no animosity but a lot of cordiality amongst the two families. It was evident that the two families approved of each other. There was not much to differentiate the two families from each other. They belonged to the same religion and had the same economic dimensions. There were no differences to contend with except in the differences in human nature and character which can cause the conflicts. But since these differences in their natures were not prominent enough, the two families gelled well. There was even talk of fixing a date for the wedding soon. Jacob and Jennifer looked at each other with a glint of joy and triumph in their eyes. The night wore off with the younger people dancing and the elderly sipping rich wine. Everyone, of course, had a grand dinner.

CHAPTER 13

Arshan leaves Sanya as the night grows old and people are stirring in their sleep. Arshan earlier took some pasta and soup which Sanya had prepared for the two of them. While bidding Sanya goodbye, Arshan pulls Sanya to him and gives her a kiss. Both of them spend the night immersed in amorous thoughts. It was a night in which the two beheld a beautiful future awaiting for them.

The day dawned, nice and beautiful. Sanya had promised the night before to meet Arshan for lunch at his home. She gets up in the morning feeling the sensations of the night before. She thought to herself that Arshan as a lover far exceeded her expectations of his sensitivity as a person. She decided that she liked Arshan in every form. She liked all of him. Sanya too had a good appetite and so had a good breakfast. She dresses up in a yellow kurta and white palazzos and leaves her house to meet Arshan for lunch. When Sanya arrives, Arshan takes Sanya on a tour of his house and the sprawling acres outside. Arshan at first shows Sanya the shooting range and for the first time reveals to Sanya his interest in shooting. " I would love to watch you shoot someday," Sanya said to Arshan. " Sure, dear," Arshan replied.

Both of them return hand in hand to the house. Sipping fruit juice, both of them enter Arshan's gymnasium and has a look around. They sit down beside the swimming pool and take bites of the starters placed before them. They have an elaborate lunch consisting of steamed rice, chappatis, dal, vegetable curry, mutton curry, chicken biryani, paneer masala curry and fish patties. On having lunch, Arshan takes Sanya up to his bedroom. " Sanya, you can take some rest," Arshan said. " Very well then," Sanya replied. Both sit down in Arshan's bed. Sanya gets out of her shoes and sits up in the bed. She moves closer to Arshan and then holds him in a close embrace. Arshan puts his arms around Sanya and holds her tight against him. " You feel like home, Arshan," Sanya cries out. " I am happy you feel that way, love. I will always keep you safe in my heart, dear," Arshan said. Arshan holds up Sanya's chin and kisses her with passion. Sanya responds in equal fervor and kisses him back. They suck each other's lips as if they would not have enough of each other; as if there would be no end to the raging passion between them. Then Sanya pulls away from Arshan and with a smile on her face uttered," I don't want it to go too fast. I want to go a bit slowly." It's perfectly okay," Arshan agreed. Arshan lies down in bed. Sanya lies down beside him and cuddles up to him. Both remain thus for sometime before sleep comes and they sleep a while. As evening ran into night, Sanya leaves Arshan for her home. Before leaving, she promises Arshan that she will go with him and meet his grandmother the next day at Arshan's ancestral home.

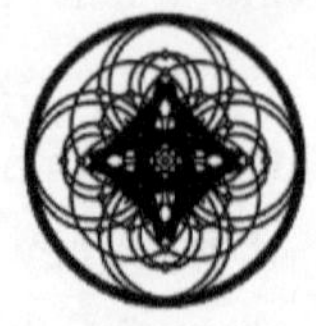

CHAPTER 14

Arshan shared a close bond with his grandmother, Parinaaz Wadia. She remained as the cornerstone of the love with which Arshan's childhood was loaded with. She would indulge in all his childhood loves and hates and regale him with bed time stories. She would solve all his childhood problems. It was Parinaaz who created for Arshan all the fairy worlds where his imagination would swim and most of the time put him to sleep. His childhood repository of fears and happiness lay with Parinaaz. Even his adult day's mischief, likes and dislikes were hidden inside his grandmother's heart. Arshan's relation with his parents was one of closeness and respect. He loved his parents with a protectiveness that was the hallmark of his relationship with his parents. Otherwise he would keep away from his parents with a sense of foreboding and with a trepidation of not to rake up the ire of his parents. Arshan had carried this sense of anxiety in regard to his parents from childhood and into his adult life. When he thought of introducing Sanya to his family, his grandmother is the one person that he knew would be the first person he wanted Sanya to meet. Arshan wanted Parinaaz to accept Sanya. He could then seek his grandmother's help in getting the approval of his parents to make Sanya his life partner. And that was what Arshan had in mind when he asked Sanya to accompany him to meet his grandmother. He thought of proposing to Sanya on a later date. Arshan felt that marriage would be the final outcome of their relationship. He did not want their relationship to be mired in a long courtship. Arshan was convinced that their love was an eternal love and marriage would definitely give it the stability it required at this early stage.

Arshan picks up Sanya from her apartment and both of them together go to meet Parinaaz Wadia. Arshan's grandmother resided in the eastern wing of the grand mansion which was the ancestral home of the Wadias. The western wing was the one which housed the rooms which were occupied by Arshan's parents. At the moment both of Arshan's parents were in Europe. The middle wing of the mansion was the one which had Arshan's rooms in it. It was also fitted with a gymnasium and the kitchen and a huge living room was situated in it. As Sanya gets down from the car and proceeds with Arshan to his house, she is struck by the grand scale in which the house had been built. It was a huge rambling house splendid enough to make one raise one's eyes in either awe at its size or stop awhile to admire its spectacular beauty. Arshan walks Sanya to the wing in which his grandmother stayed.

Parinaaz Wadia was waiting for the arrival of her grandson. She had taken extra care today to get ready and meet her grandson's lady love. She was joyous that she will be meeting Arshan after an interval of two months. She had so much to say to Arshan. Again, Arshan had surprised her yesterday by talking to her about Sanya. This was the first time Parinaaz had heard Arshan speak so fondly of a woman and especially wanted to bring a woman home to meet her. Parinaaz could sense the happiness in her grandson's voice. She could feel that Arshan was surely in love. This thought made her more excited to meet Sanya. She wanted to see the woman who had captured her most loved grandson's heart. Parinaaz eagerly awaited their arrival.

Arshan and Sanya arrive and greet Parinaaz. Parinaaz is taken up by the beautiful Sanya and her polite, sweet manners. She felt in those very first moments that both Arshan and Sanya complimented each other in beauty and in temperament. Parinaaz could see that a quiet girl like Sanya could provide the much needed stability and companionship to Arshan's hectic and lonely life. Parinaaz knew for certain that it was lonely being on top of the ladder in a company. You are solely responsible for your decisions. A girl like Sanya could fill the void in Arshan's life. At the end of the day, Parinaaz was happy with the way Sanya was and so indicated to Arshan that she approved of his choice.

CHAPTER 15

On the way home, Arshan convinced Sanya to accompany him to London for a week. Sanya agreed, after being coaxed by Arshan, to take leave from office and go with him to London. Sanya was somewhat excited at the prospect of going to a foreign land. She had never been abroad before. The excitement lay in not only witnessing an unknown country but also in the thought of love unfolding between the couple in ways unbeknownst to them. Sanya and Arshan knew that this journey to be undertaken would lay the foundations of something beautiful and solid. It would lay out their relationship for the future and would give them a sense of where they stand with each other in subsequent times. Sanya is fully convinced that Arshan would keep her and her heart safe.

Arshan and Sanya arrive in London aboard Arshan's chartered plane. They immediately drive to the house where Arshan lived. Sanya is shown into her room by the house keeper. She is trying to settle down when Arshan enters her room and tells her that they would meet each other at lunch time. He asks Sanya to tell Mrs Williams, the house keeper, if she needs anything. Sanya unpacks her things and arranges her clothes and shoes in the cupboards. She then takes her bath and lies down in bed as she waits for lunch time to come. Sanya meets Arshan at lunch. Arshan says," Tomorrow I am taking you on a tour of the company. We will leave at about thirty minutes to nine o'clock in the morning. It is a thirty minutes drive to the company. You can have a look around and come back for lunch." "Won't you come back with me for lunch," Sanya asks Arshan. " No dear. But I will take you out in the evening," Arshan replied. " Where are we going in the evening," Sanya asks. Arshan says," I have not decided so far. We will go out for a movie or a drive and we will dine out." " That is fine," Sanya says. After lunch, Arshan takes leave of Sanya and goes out to his office.

The night arrives and the couple have dinner together. Arshan kisses Sanya goodnight and as the couple are about to retire to their rooms for the night, Sanya embraces Arshan and leans her head against his chest. She puts up her face and looking at him sleepily says, " I don't want to be alone." Arshan smiles at her and lifting her in his arms, carries her to his bedroom. He carefully lays her in bed. He then lies down beside Sanya and as Sanya lay on her side, Arshan quietly presses his body against her. On such a peaceful note, both soon fall asleep. Both of them are exhausted by the long journey they had taken from India.

Arshan gets up in the morning and finds Sanya sleeping soundly beside him. He softly gets out of bed and without waking up Sanya goes off to do a bit of running. Running a few miles in the morning clears Arshan's mind and it removes all the clogs that might beset his mind depriving his ability to think clearly and soundly. Sanya gets up and finds Arshan gone. She returns to her room and refreshes herself. She sees Arshan for a little while during breakfast. Both of them leave for the factory. Arshan shows Sanya the factory and at lunch time Sanya comes back to the house. Arshan asks her to get ready by six o'clock in the evening so that both of them could go out for a movie. As the evening draws near, Sanya gets ready for the evening outing. Arshan arrives home in time and along with Sanya leaves to see the movie. For Sanya, the movie she sees is almost a blur. It is the sense of togetherness, she feels with her lover, that engrosses her. It is exhilarating when she and Arshan embark on a long drive after the movie is over. As the night dawns they stop by and have dinner at a fancy restaurant. The couple is in a daze as to their time spent together. There is a feeling of contentment together with the immense feeling of love and care both now feel for each other. A feeling of nurturing arose in them.

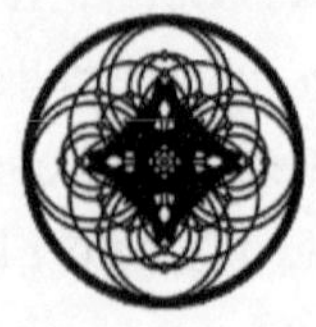

CHAPTER 16

Arshan decides to take a break from work and take Sanya on a three day tour of the Scottish Highlands. Sanya had inquired about the place. Arshan had come to know of Sanya's love for scenic beauty. Sanya was joyous at Arshan's suggestion that they pay a visit to Scotland. Both boarded the flight in the evening and landed in Edinburgh before nightfall. They decided to start for the Highlands the next day after breakfast. Sanya lay in Arshan's arms as they slept in the night in a hotel in Edinburgh. Sanya, while going to sleep, twined her arms and legs around Arshan's and would not let him go during the night. The couple gets into a car in the morning and drives off to the Highlands. They preferred the journey by car as they would then be able to feast their eyes on the ensuing breathtakingly beautiful landscape. Arshan had rented a villa in Inverness and after a journey of almost three hours through the beauteous sights, the couple reach the place. They disembark from the car and after taking a shower immediately have lunch. They were definitely hungry after the long drive. The joy in their hearts seemed to enhance their appetite. The couple take rest after lunch is over.

In the evening, the couple would walk hand in hand through the streets of the city taking in the sights and sounds of the city. Arshan's spirit soared amidst the anonymity he enjoyed together with a sense of belonging to his beloved. Sanya was elated beyond words with Arshan there to love her and take care of her. She felt a sense of freedom with him. Arshan seemed to have opened up her mind and incited her to new ways of thinking. She had started to explore new ideas which she constricted her mind not to follow otherwise but held them back as sacrilegious things. She was extremely happy. As the night came on, the couple had their dinner in a local inn. They take a cab back to the villa.

Arshan and Sanya get back to the villa. They go up to their room. As the two lovers change into their night clothes, Sanya comes out from the washroom and sees Arshan pulling out his shirt. She slowly approaches Arshan and then runs to him. She puts her arms around him and holds him in a tight embrace from the back. Sanya kisses him on his back several times. Arshan leans back against Sanya. Both stay on in this way for sometime savouring in the moment. Arshan then turns around and takes Sanya in his arms. He kisses her lips deeply. As Arshan lets go of Sanya, she slips out of her nightgown and stands before Arshan. Arshan pulls out his trousers and holds Sanya very close to him. As their bodies meet, fire rages through them and they breath heavily. They kiss each other again and again. Arshan lays down Sanya in bed. He kisses her forehead, her lips, her neck and then each of her breasts. Sanya cries out," I love you." " I love you too, baby," Arshan responds. " Shall I come in," Arshan asks Sanya." Yes dear," Sanya replies. Arshan pushes open Sanya's legs and comes inside of her. Sanya gasps as she feels for the first time a pain mingled with pleasure. Arshan at first is slow and soft in his movements and then his passion takes over and his love making becomes more intense. Sanya holds on to

Arshan like a lifeline. Both of them reach the pinnacle of their ecstacy together. As both of them lie in bed holding each other, Arshan says," Was it alright?" " You are just perfect," Sanya told Arshan. As the passionate, amorous night slowly draws to an end, the couple fall into deep sleep.

CHAPTER 17

Sanya opens her eyes to find Arshan sleeping peacefully by her side. She smiles and lightly kisses him on the lips. Arshan opens his eyes and smiles back at Sanya. The night before of love and intensity had brought a soft glow into both their beings leaving them feeling happy and satisfied. A happiness which had a touch of heavenly bliss to it.

The happy couple set out to explore the rugged mountains and the famous lochs of Scotland. They took a walk to the Ness Islands through one of the suspension bridges. Then they visited the famous loch " Loch Ness" and admired its stunning beauty. They witness nature in all its glory; nothing fancy but raw and infectious which melt their hearts. This combined with the love in their hearts made the experience anything but magical.

Arshan and Sanya spent the last day in Scotland in the villa at Inverness. Both of them sleep till the morning in each other's embrace. Sanya gets up from bed after kissing Arshan on the lips. Arshan lies on his back and sleeps some more. After taking breakfast, both walk around in the garden which lay about the villa. They sit outside in the sun for some time and take in the beautiful weather that graced the day. As the evening gets colder both of them have soup and crackers and curl up together in the living room sofa. Arshan reads out some French poetry to Sanya explaining to her the meaning of the words and the sentences. Sanya cuddles up to Arshan and lying on his chest listens, with rapt attention and with admiration, to the words which espoused love or which described nature in all its glory. Arshan had learnt French while on a one year long trip in France. He was doing internship in a French company. His evenings were idle; either spent in the theatres or was spent drinking and conversing with friends. It was one of his friends who recited some French poetry which piqued his interest in learning and acquiring the language. He started to attend a French language class in an Institute run by an elderly lady in the evenings. He did a six month course in the French language. Although six months is not enough to gain proficiency over a language yet Arshan's extensive reading of French literature increased and honed his skills in the language. Though he did not attain mastery over the language yet he became good at it. Sanya, an avid reader herself, was hardly much into reading poetry. She read English literature widely but she always thought of poetry as esoteric and did not enjoy it much. Since she did not enjoy it much, Sanya did not try to get into the depth of English poetry. But now she loved the way Arshan read out poetry as also his descriptions of the poet's visions and their beauteous notions.

The night came on and as Sanya embrace Arshan amorously, Arshan says," You have to tell me what you want, my love." Sanya smiles and holding Arshan tight she says," I want you, all of you." Arshan pulls her tight against him and kisses her deeply. He gropes for Sanya's clothes and removes her nightgown. He kisses her neck and licks the skin in between her breasts. Sanya trembles with the passion that is slowly consuming her. Arshan takes each of Sanya's breasts in his mouth and sucks them. Sanya heaves with pleasure and cries out. Arshan slowly moves his tongue down Sanya's stomach and nibbles her navel. He then moves down to the place in between her legs and kisses her warm, throbbing, hidden pleasure point. Sanya cries out to Arshan," Come inside. Please come inside," Arshan lightly pushes Sanya to bed and then lowers himself to her. Pushing open her legs, he goes inside her. Their mutual movements and their voracious craving for each other's bodies cause them to orgasm. They hold each other and sleep for the night.

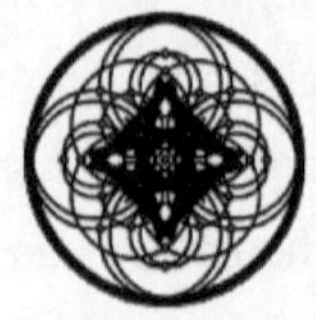

CHAPTER 18

Arshan and Sanya were to leave Scotland for London in the afternoon. In the morning, Sanya gets up to find that Arshan had already woken up and was not present in the room. She at once gets up, takes a shower and gets ready for breakfast. Arshan comes into the bedroom and addresses Sanya," Good morning. I see you are wide awake and up and going." " Good morning," Sanya says and smiles at Arshan. Arshan pulls out a small box from his trouser pocket and opens it. It has an exquisitely carved diamond ring in it. He takes out the ring and walks towards Sanya. He takes Sanya's hand and then puts the ring in her finger. Sanya looks at him with surprise in her eyes. " I want you to wear this ring always. It is a symbol of our love. And I might as well say that we are engaged from today," Arshan said to Sanya. He pulls Sanya to him and kisses her. With tears in her eyes, Sanya embraces Arshan and utters," Oh, I am so happy."

The couple arrives in London at nightfall. They have dinner and the exhausting journey makes them sleep easily. Sanya spent the next day walking in the garden of the house and taking in the sun. It was a beautiful day. Sanya breathed in the fresh air. The beauty of the day was enhanced by the sense of joy Sanya felt inside of her. She day dreamed of a life full of abundance and joy with Arshan by her side. Arshan comes back from office early to spend the rest of the day with Sanya. Sanya was to leave for India the next day.

Sanya leaves for India with mixed feelings of joy and sadness. Leaving Arshan made her sad but the prospect of marriage with Arshan and spending a lifetime with him made her ecstatic. Sanya on landing in India comes to the realization that she would now have to talk to her parents and convince them of her decision to marry Arshan. Meanwhile Arshan calls up his grandmother and informs her of his decision to accept Sanya as his life partner. He seeks Parinaaz Wadia's help to convince his parents to accept his choice of a life partner.

Both the families agree to the marriage of Arshan and Sanya. Sanya's father had initial reservations about the marriage. He was apprehensive about the newness of everything his daughter would have to face in this marriage including all the cultural, community and class differences. But when he saw that his daughter was very much in love with Arshan, he agreed to the match. It was decided that the marriage would be solemnized in Mumbai. It was also decided that Arshan would pay a visit to the Bharadwaj family in Varanasi before the marriage.

Arshan slowly wraps up his work in London or rather he leaves his responsibility at the hands of others for the time being. He thought that it is more appropriate to get his personal life going at this time. Arshan leaves London exactly one month after Sanya's departure from London. Arshan lands in Varanasi and is met at the airport by Sanya and her father. Arshan would stay the night in Varanasi before flying off to Mumbai the next day. The Bharadwaj family goes all out in their attempt at entertaining the guest and making him feel comfortable. Arshan feels awkward and is irritated at all these attempts by everyone to please him. He hides his displeasure and mingles with the members of the Bharadwaj family. Sanya could sense Arshan's uneasiness but could hardly do anything to contain her over enthusiastic family members. In the evening Arshan along with Sanya goes for a walk along the river Ganges. Both walk in silence savouring in the quiet, holy spirit of the city.

It was decided on this day that Arshan and Sanya would get married twenty days hence. Sanya agrees to resign from her job in order to live with Arshan in London. Arshan would have to stay some more time in London to finish the unfinished business of amalgamating the company with his company in India. He wanted the two companies to retain their separate identities in spite of the amalgamation but they have to be under one umbrella. Arshan bids goodbye to the Bharadwaj family and leaves Varanasi for Mumbai in the morning.

CHAPTER 19

Sanya was staying with her parents in Varanasi when Arshan had landed in Mumbai. Arshan meets his parents after visiting Sanya's place in Varanasi. Both Arshan and his parents discuss the forthcoming marriage. On Arshan's request Parinaaz had impressed upon her son and daughter in law about the suitability of Sanya as Arshan's bride. She recounted her meeting with Sanya and Arshan. She enumerated the sterling qualities of goodness, calmness and poise that Sanya possessed. She told them that Sanya would be an ideal bride for Arshan. Both Adel and Tanaz knew that they can rely on Parinaaz's sense of judgement but they also knew that Parinaaz could be blinded sometimes by her love for Arshan. Sensing this they told Arshan that they would like to meet Sanya. Sanya was to leave for Mumbai with her parents and some other relatives for her wedding a week before her the wedding day. But she had to leave her home earlier as Arshan expressed his parent's desire to meet her.

Arshan picks up Sanya and both of them are driven to Arshan's ancestral home. Sanya is nervous to meet Arshan's parents. She was afraid that they might not take a liking to her. She herself did not know where this anxiety came from for she had not felt like this when she met Parinaaz Wadia. Then she was very confident. It was the way Parinaaz treated her with love and understanding that made her feel that she could make Arshan's family her own. Arshan and Sanya reach the Wadias family residence to find that Adel and Tanaz were waiting from them. Arshan's parents were sitting in the chairs laid out in the lawn of the house. Sanya greets them. Adel and Tanaz invite her to sit with them. As the four of them sit and talk, the concerns that Adel and Tanaz had about their future daughter in law seemed to fade away. Adel especially was happy that Sanya was a much grounded person. Sanya too felt that Adel and Tanaz were a loveable couple.

As the couple wait for their marriage to take place, Sanya falls ill. It is night time and Jennifer finds out that Sanya is suffering from high fever. Sanya lies in bed almost unable to speak. Jennifer gives Sanya a tablet to reduce the fever. Sanya swallows the tablet. But after a time when the fever shows no sign of abetment, Jennifer panics. She picks up the phone and calls Arshan. Arshan tells Jennifer to stay calm. He tells her that he is on his way to the apartment. Arshan reaches the apartment and finding Sanya burning with fever, he immediately asks Jennifer for a bowl of water and a piece of cloth. As Jennifer hands him the things Arshan had asked for, he soaks the cloth in water and places it on Sanya's forehead. He keeps on doing this every few minutes and slowly after about forty five minutes Sanya's fever subsides. Both Jennifer and Arshan are relieved. Arshan tells Jennifer that he would stay back at the apartment and look after Sanya. He asks Jennifer to take some rest. Arshan spends the whole night lying down in a sofa in Sanya's bedroom. He would get up now and then to check on Sanya. In the early hours of the morning as sleep overcomes Arshan, he hears Sanya calling out to him. He goes to Sanya's side. Sanya looks at him and gives him a weak smile. Arshan smiles at Sanya and taking her hand in his says," You scared me a little, dear." As the morning goes up and Jennifer is out of bed and Sanya gets better, Arshan leaves the two women and heads for his home.

The Bharadwaj family travelled to Mumbai ten days before the wedding of Sanya and Arshan. Sanya's parents, brother and sister and a number of her aunts, uncles and cousins had come to Mumbai to attend the wedding. Sanya's parents, brother and sister stayed with Sanya and Jennifer at their apartment. Makeshift beds were set up in the living room of the apartment for the family to sleep in. The other relatives stayed in a hotel which was booked by Arshan. Arshan's family bore much of the expenses of the wedding. The class differences between the two families were all too pronounced. The way they talked, their way of dressing highlighted the differences all too well. But both the families were gracious enough to accommodate the other so that there was no feeling of ill will among the members of the two families. The happiness of the bride and the groom was all that mattered to the two families. If the couple could bond so well so could they.

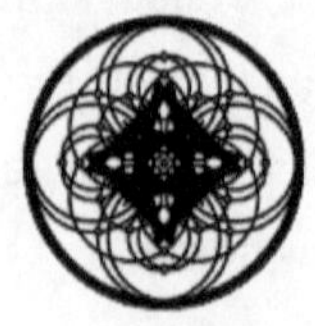

CHAPTER 20

Arshan and Sanya officially become a couple as their marriage took place in Mumbai amidst much joy and fanfare. The wedding celebrations had lasted three long days. On the wedding night, Sanya crashes into Arshan's arms as he comes into the bedroom. The couple embrace and both of them sleep peacefully with happiness and contentment writ large on their faces. They felt that they were soul mates. They felt that their union was divinely guided.

The couple leave for Italy to spend a week in Venice. Sanya expressed her desire to see the canals that flow through the city and Arshan had lovingly obliged. The couple experiences the invigorating climate of the city and Sanya especially marvels at the majestic architecture of the magnificent structures that dotted the city. They bask in the warmth of the golden sun as they lie in each other's arms and take a gondola ride through the canals of the city. The nights of the couple was consumed by endless passion. Both of them cannot get enough of the other. Their slow burning passion had reached its zenith in this wondrous city. Every night Arshan would take Sanya in his arms and pressing his body against hers would kiss her till his body became limp with desire. He would then explore her in ways which enhanced her passion to an extent to which she thought was not possible. Sanya and Arshan lapped up each other as if there was no time to live anymore and they wanted to delve in all their unmuted desires in these few days. They wound up their Venetian trip and reach London to settle into a life of happy matrimony.

The couple continued to stay in the house which Arshan occupied during his earlier stay. Sanya was diffident in the beginning as she was not familiar with the ways of the English staff which mostly comprised the household staff at the house. She tutored herself to pick up the nuances of the ways of the English people in the workforce. She slowly develops a liking for Kamala Singh, an Indian employee whom Arshan had assigned the task of looking after Sanya's household needs. Kamala is a woman in her early fifties and lived in the house. She is of Indian origin and her family which includes her only son and his family reside in Bristol. She had lost her husband early on in her marriage. She took up different jobs to support herself and her son. Kamala was a motherly figure. When she saw Sanya struggling with the foreign ways of life, she always came forward and lent the support so that Sanya coped quite easily in a short period of time. Sanya leaned on Kamala to help her arrive into her own in London. Sanya knew that this was the support she could not expect from Arshan. Arshan remained too busy with his work to help Sanya in different ways. Kamala became her support system during these initial days. And so developed this unlikely closeness between the two women.

Sanya after basking a couple of months as a new bride in a new household was slowly growing restless. Boredom had taken the place of novelty. She felt she was leading a barren existence; one in which she felt lonely when her husband was away from home and was happy in his presence. She alternated between utter desolation and immense happiness. She wanted to have more balance in her emotions. She wanted to be engaged in something fruitful. She talked about it with Arshan. Arshan asked Sanya to join his company. Sanya was not very inclined to work in Arshan's company or in any other company. She thought of doing a course in creative writing. She told Arshan of her idea. Arshan readily agreed. He wanted Sanya to keep herself busy and remain as happy as can be. Sanya got admission into a course in creative writing in a college in London.

Every day after breakfast, Arshan would drop Sanya at the college and then would himself be driven to work. Although Arshan arranged for a car to pick up Sanya when her classes were over, Sanya had other ideas. She told Arshan that she wanted to come home on her own. Arshan, though not happy with the suggestion, agreed to Sanya's pleadings. Sanya wanted to explore the city of London alone. She would sometimes walk around the city after her classes were over and then take the Tube back to her home. In other days she would get on a cab and be driven home. She went visiting the British museum and spent half a day gazing at the displays in the museum. She took a tour of the Buckingham Palace. Another day she went to the Tower Bridge and looked for a long time at the Thames river. She was fascinated by the city of London. At night as she lay in Arshan's arms, she would recall for him all she had seen and done during the day. Arshan would lovingly stroke her body as he listened to her. He was happy that Sanya was slowly settling into this life with him.

Sanya gets news from Jennifer that Jennifer's marriage has been fixed with Jacob. Jennifer invites both Arshan and Sanya to her marriage. The marriage is to be solemnized in Goa. Sanya is excited and happy for her friend. She tells Arshan that they should attend the wedding. Arshan being too busy with the restructuring work of his company tells Sanya of his preoccupation with his work. He, however, asks Sanya to attend her friend's wedding. Sanya would have to go alone to India to attend Jennifer's wedding; yet she was happy at the prospect of seeing her friends again. Jennifer had informed Sanya that Anita would be attending the wedding ceremony. Sanya missed her friends; the earthiness and the solace she had found in Jennifer and the fun and mischievousness of Anita. The goodwill shared by each one of them for the other was the cause of a lasting bond between the three friends. Sanya gets ready to leave for India. She would land in Mumbai, take rest for a day in her home in Mumbai and then embark on her journey to Goa. Sanya gets to Goa and goes off straight to meet Jennifer at her home. Jennifer's house is decorated with white and orange flowers and fairy lights and with red and yellow clothes draped around the pillars and the railings of the staircase. Sanya and Anita watch as Jennifer gets decked up as the quintessential Christian bride. Jennifer wears a flowing white gown with flowers embroidered on it. She wears a floral band on her head and lets her hair loose. She looks radiant and beautiful. She looks bright and happy. Sanya wears a mauve coloured dress and Anita wears a light yellow coloured dress. The two ladies look attractive and with the wedding spirit infused into them they look alluring. As the guests take their place in the church, Jacob dressed in a suit and a bow tie waits the arrival of the bride. Jennifer is led up the aisle by her father. With the priest in attendance, the bride and the groom take their vows and the priest pronounces Jacob and Jennifer as husband and wife. The wedding being over in the morning, the feast for the guests takes place in the evening. It is a beach party and everyone enjoys the drinks and the food that is laid out. Sanya and Anita catches up with the events that dominate their lives at the moment. They are happy to be reunited with each other after a long time. They seemed once again to relive their days spent in Mumbai. A day after the wedding is over Sanya leaves Mumbai for London. Sanya missed Arshan and wanted to be back with him in London.

CHAPTER 21

Sanya would often see Amanda Baker cycling to college to catch up with her classes. Amanda was a student of creative writing in Sanya's class. She was a lovely young woman with blonde hair. She was tall and walked with a gait which made her look as if she swayed from side to side. Sanya loved the simple ways of life. She loved the fact that Amanda always cycled to college. She also loved the way Amanda conducted herself; confidently, courteously. She was friendly and non judgemental. Sanya became acquainted with Amanda while both were having lunch at the college restaurant. Sanya came to know that Amanda was the mother of a one year old baby boy. Her husband, George Baker was a high school teacher in a school in London. Amanda and George lived in a rented apartment in London. Every morning George would drive his boy to the crèche and drop him there before driving off to the school to take his classes. Amanda would quickly finish up her household work and then cycle to the college for her classes. In the evening George would again bring his boy from the crèche to his home.

Sanya and Amanda became very good friends. They discussed books, music, their personal lives as also their dreams for the future. It was Amanda who introduced the different types of English music into Sanya's life; be it folk music, classical music or popular music. In India Sanya did listen to some of the popular English music. But she was a new entrant into the world of English folk and classical music. Sanya and Amanda would together go shopping to the music shops in search of music albums which Sanya would then buy. The type of music and the artists were recommended by Amanda. Sanya, when she listened to the music, always thought Amanda had good taste. Amanda would sometimes lend Sanya some of her music albums. The two friends often discussed about books and their authors. If Sanya was an admirer of the books of Thomas Hardy, Amanda was a lover of the books by Jane Austen. Amanda liked books with magic realism as the theme. Sanya liked books of the romantic genre. Both loved detective novels.

One day when Amanda travelled to college on the Tube, she invited Sanya to her home. Sanya felt cozy and happy in Amanda's small home. She felt an enveloping love in Amanda and George's home; a home created by the love of George and Amanda. Sanya felt that the small, happy home of George, Amanda and their child was all that one would crave for. She for once wanted Arshan to be less busy with his work. She wanted him to be more often at home. She wanted to bear his child. She wanted to create a happy home like the one Amanda had created and had protected it with love and commitment. Amanda offered Sanya tea and some home made cookies and cake. Sanya and Amanda had tea and talked for a long time into the evening. Arshan, when he came home and found that Sanya was at her friend's home, sent the car to bring her home. Sanya came home with joy in her heart and related to Arshan all the things that impressed her about the Baker family. On Sanya's request, one evening Amanda visits Sanya's home for tea. Amanda marvels at the beauty of the huge house. She admires the way Sanya has decorated the whole house. While she extolled the house, Amanda thought of her small, peaceful home she had made with George and she knew she would prefer to be nowhere but in her own home. Amanda had found her happiness in her life with George by her side.

Amanda and George grew up in a village called Abbotsbury which is situated in the English county of Dorset. They were childhood friends. Friendship blossomed into love as they grew up. They got married after they had completed their graduation. Amanda invites Sanya to stay with her in Abbotsbury during the summer holidays. Sanya acquires Arshan's consent to go on the journey. Sanya, Amanda, George and baby Jorgan take the four and half hour journey from London to Abbotsbury by train. Sanya takes the seat near to the window and her eyes remain fixated to the beautiful scenery outside of that window as the train rolled out. As the train rolled on so did the scenery outside changed every few minutes. It was magical and Sanya was fascinated. When they reached the village Sanya could see that it was surrounded by hills on three sides. It comprised of a long street with stone houses and after a few miles the street opened into a market square. Life went on at a silent and steady pace in this small village. Life was just so simple. Amanda and George lived in a stone house with a small garden at the back of the house. The house is owned by George's mother. She had grown tomatoes, cucumbers, beans in the garden. Sanya stayed in this house with the family. Every morning Sanya would help George's mother make breakfast for the family. Sanya being an amicable person, the elderly lady grew fond of her. In the noon time as Amanda prepared lunch for all, Sanya would take care of little Jorgan. Sanya would sometimes accompany George to get some supplies from the market. The days spent in that small village made Sanya happy. It made her think that life could be so idyllic. Meanwhile in London Arshan started to miss Sanya. He all of a sudden decides to give his wife a surprise and travel to Abbotsbury. As he sets foot in Amanda and George's house, Sanya is thrilled and flies into his arms. George helps Arshan find out a house which Arshan hires. Arshan and Sanya spend a week in this house. Sanya is all too happy to indulge in her culinary skills and prepare food for Arshan as well as look after all his needs. The couple return to London after spending seven blissful days in Abbotsbury.

CHAPTER 22

It is six months into their marriage and Sanya discovers that she is pregnant. The couple is happy. Sanya insists on continuing her classes at the college. Arshan allows her to go on with her classes but forbids her from coming home on her own. He makes sure that a car picks her up when her classes get over. Sanya is happy that something of Arshan is inside of her now. She wants to nurture it lovingly and bring it into this world with pride and joy. She would touch her womb now and then and smile with a lot of contentment. In these moments she would think about Arshan and feel all over again the love that encompasses their relationship. After Sanya conceived, Arshan made it a habit to call up Sanya several times during the day. It at times irritated Sanya. She was by this time quite used to being on her own all day. And this nervous attention from Arshan got her a little worked up at times. There was a time when she first came to London that she wanted all of Arshan's attention. But when she did not get it, Sanya churned up her own devices to keep herself busy and animated. She did not blame Arshan. She knew he was short on time and that she had to look after herself.

Sanya had struck up an easy friendship with Kamala. She

would often sit with her and converse on different topics. Sanya found that Kamala had an active mind and kept abreast of the political events and the social trends. She also read books and that was what was so attractive to Sanya. Sanya could grow fond of even a stranger if one loved books. For she herself loved books and always found life brimming in these books. So many characters in these books has given shape to her own thinking, has opened her eyes to the realities and the complexities of life. So many a time she had forgotten her own dilemmas as she delved into the intricacies of these character's lives. It was seldom that a book or some part of it did not touch her.

Sanya continued to attend the creative writing classes at the college through her pregnancy. But five months into her pregnancy, the doctors asked her to take rest at home and to avoid travel as much as possible. It was decided that Sanya would stop attending her classes and stay at home. After Arshan kissed Sanya goodbye after breakfast, Sanya would spend most of the day watching television or movies or she would read extensively. Sometimes she would just idle away her time by sitting in the front porch and looking out into the garden. A lot many ideas would strike her at those times. She could visualize the many characters and then she would put them in settings of her imagination. Some characters would flourish and many others would vanish as vapour rises from a pot of boiling water and then disappears from vision. One fine day Sanya decided to catch hold of these characters floating about in her mind and bring them into existence. She decided to write. Sanya started putting down her thoughts on paper. She became ambitious and made up her mind to write a full fledged novel. Her mind conjured up the outline of a story. She thought she knew the beginning and the end of the story. So when she had the basic structure of the story, she decided to embellish it with flesh and blood. She resolved to put up the framework of her story and fill up the gaps in between. Sanya talked to Arshan about her decision. He encouraged her to go ahead and do her writing. He, of course, reminded her to take it easy and not to stress out too much. Sanya started writing and a sense of freedom enveloped her whole being as if she was releasing some pent up emotions from her person. She was happy now and for most of the time afterwards as she felt that she was expending her mind in doing something she absolutely revelled in.

Meanwhile Anita writes to Sanya that she was getting married to Ajay Shroff. Ajay Shroff was a businessman and a non resident Indian. He resided in Canada with his family. Anita and Ajay's father were childhood friends. Each one thought of the other when their children came to be of marriageable age. They thought that a marriage alliance between their children would be a wonderful thing. The two friends had set up a meeting between Anita and Ajay. As per his father's wishes Ajay lands in Mumbai to meet up with Anita. Ajay is a tall, lanky man who is fair and has a bearded look. He is not exactly handsome but his tall, lithe figure more than compensates for his looks. He is a man with a definite impressive personality. The first time Ajay and Anita lay their eyes on each other, they form a special bond. Their bond is formed not out of an overwhelming sense of love but out of friendship. Besides the likeness of the things they believed in made them all the more sure of entering the matrimonial bond. Anita and Ajay met each other for a period of two weeks. There was no any extended courtship for the couple as in the third week Ajay's family came down to India to plan for the marriage. The couple had decided to get married. Sanya expressed her inability to attend the marriage as she was confined. She gave her best wishes to the couple. Anita and Ajay got married on the fourth week of Ajay landing in India. Anita gave up her job and accompanied Ajay to live with him in Canada.

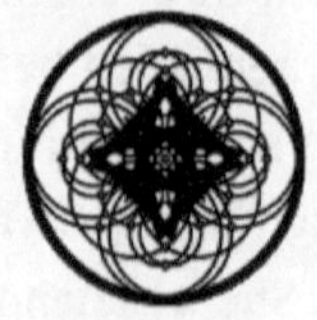

CHAPTER 23

Sanya is entering the eighth month of her pregnancy. She still writes regularly and is half way through writing her novel. Then one day all of a sudden she feels the pangs of labour pain. She is taken to the hospital and with Arshan by her side she gives birth to twins- a boy and a girl. They name the boy, Farzan and the girl, Meher. The giggling of the tiny babies filled the house with enormous joy and contentment. The couple always argue as to whom the babies resemble; whether they resemble their father or their mother. Arshan is so happy that he even changes the babies' nappies when he is at home. He would carry the two little ones in the crook of each of his arms. He would even sing to them. Sanya is amused to see this side of Arshan. She had often wondered what kind of a father Arshan would be. She was delighted to see him play with the babies and take care of them. Sanya had grown up with a father who was always available for the children right from when they were kids till they needed him in later life. Suraj Bharadwaj looked after his children's physical and emotional needs all too well. Sanya idolized her father. And now when she finds Arshan taking care of his two small babies, she is joyous.

Sanya and Arshan watch as their two babies grow up and slowly gain the strength to stand up on their feet. They could never get tired of seeing their antics. Farzan was the quiet one and Meher, the boisterous one. Both the children would noisily play on as Sanya would watch over them and write on her study table. She had moved her study table to the bedroom so that she could write as well as look after the children. Sanya loved to write amidst the noise and chatter of her two children. She always needed some noise in the background so as to concentrate on her writing. Earlier she used to play some music in the room she was writing in or she would leave the television on. Silence did not appeal to her. Silence had a sense of foreboding. Some noise created a lively atmosphere to write in. Sanya had started writing after two months of the twins' birth. She had also resumed her classes in the college. While going for the classes she would leave her children in the care of their English governess.

The atmosphere at home was one of harmonious existence. Arshan and Sanya loved each other and their two babies were a testimony of their love for each other. They dreamed the same dreams. They wanted their children to grow up well and go into the world and find love and happiness as they themselves had found in each other.

CHAPTER 24

The children are now one and half years old. Sanya had completed her studies and had taken her degree in creative writing. Arshan was almost finishing his unfinished business with his newly acquired British company. He along with his team had successfully amalgamated the company with his Indian company. Arshan has a talk with Sanya. Arshan wanted to know and also decide when to return to his home country. Sanya convinced him that this was the right time to leave for India. Sanya told Arshan that she loved his house in Mumbai. Sanya told him that she wanted to bring up her children in that house. This affirmation from Sanya for returning to India made it easy for Arshan to decide to return to his country.

Arshan and Sanya wrap up their life in London and return to Mumbai. They slowly settle into their life in Mumbai. Arshan is usually busy with his work schedule at the company. Though he is devoted to his wife and children, he has so less time to spend with his family. Sanya was left on her own to utilize her time and spend it in ways of her own. She spent most of her time writing. She wanted to complete the book she had started to write back in London. It was only in the night that the couple saw each other. It was the only time that they conversed with each other and had some meaningful dialogues. It was at night that Arshan took Sanya in his arms and made love to her night after night. After their love making the two of them would sleep hugging each other. Sanya got to see Arshan during breakfast in the morning when he would kiss her on the forehead and go out for the day.

Arshan, after having finished restructuring of the British company that he took over, wanted to bring vast changes to the company that he owned in India. He wanted to modernize the company. He wanted the company to diversify into various fields other than steel. He wanted the company to enter into sectors as diverse as telecommunication, textiles, information technology and the retail sector. Arshan had already brought in some changes in the company when he took charge of the company for a short span of time during his father's illness. He now wanted to bring in sweeping changes in the company. He wanted the company to grow manifold. Arshan had a talk with his father about his plans for the company. His father supported him and he believed in Arshan's sense of judgement regarding his vision for the company. Adel's close associate, Jehangir, whom Arshan addressed as uncle since his childhood was not very agreeable to Arshan's plans. Jehangir was opposed to the idea of laying off a large number of the workers in the process of modernizing the company. The two men discussed the matter for sometime but could not come to an amicable decision. At the end of the discussion a frustrated Arshan said to Jehangir," You are slowing me down." This remark upset Jehangir so much that he took the decision to resign from the Board of Directors. Jehangir felt hurt as he always thought that he had all his life worked for the betterment of the company. His resignation gave Arshan a freehand to deal with the other directors and to persuade them to agree to his plans which in due course he did.

Sanya finishes her book and re-reads the whole manuscript once again. She readies the book to be sent to the publishers. She sends her book to a number of publishing houses. All but one publisher accepts her book for publishing. Sanya is happy at the first taste of success. Arshan accompanies her to the book launch party. Sanya's book is a success. She had to go on a book signing and book reading spree across the country. The publisher draws up a list of the important cities where Sanya's book needs to be promoted. The cities included Delhi, Mumbai, Kolkata, Bangalore, Chennai and Hyderabad. Besides the big cities, they also included smaller cities like Pune, Meerut, Varanasi, Jaipur. Sanya would have to travel to these cities and promote her book by appearing in discussions on the book, by reading the chapters of her book to an audience and by signing copies of her book which were bought by the book reading public. Sanya's confidence in herself is boosted as she travels alone to the different cities for the promotion of her book. The book is received well by the public and she also gets good reviews from the critics. Sanya slowly become a darling of the book readers in the country. Of the cities she visited, Sanya found Kolkata the most impressive. She finds the city interspersed with the old British colonial buildings and the new modern ones. The presence of both these old and new structures fascinated her. She found the people that she met in Kolkata to be very enthusiastic and aware about their culture and their roots. They took conscious and at times unconscious pride in their culture. She loved the varieties of Bengali sweets; roshogolla, sandesh and sweet yogurt known as mishti doi. She partook of the many different preparations of fish curries and liked them a lot.

Sanya completes her book promotion tour and comes home.

She is reunited with her family. She is most happy to be amongst her children but misses Arshan a lot. When she is in his arms at night, she tells him," I miss you a lot, dear. Can't you be at home more often." " I will try to," Arshan says. " Sanya, lets go on a holiday for some days to a nearby hill station. Let us take the children too. Let us be together for some time." " Yes, that's a very good idea, Arshan. We could relax a bit then," Sanya says to Arshan.

The couple decides to visit Shimla, a small hill station in the abode of the Himalayas. They decide to go to Shimla on a Sunday and spend a week there.

CHAPTER 25

It is September and the winter season has commenced in Shimla. The weather is cool and lovely. Snow has not yet started to fall in here. Arshan, Sanya and their two children along with the children's governess reach Shimla and put up in a hotel out there. The couple feel relaxed in this holistic atmosphere. Their minds are set at rest. Their proximity to the serene beauty of nature; Arshan's move away from his routine business schedule and Sanya's end of her hectic book promotion tour were reason for the calming effect on their frayed nerves. The children, a bit perturbed in the first few hours by the sudden change of place were calmed by the soothing words of their mother and the playful attitude of their governess. They forgot their anxiety when they started to play.

In the afternoon, after the couple had lunch, Arshan had an urgent call from London. Following the call, Arshan had to do an emergency video conference with the London based directors of his company. A labour problem which was brewing up for some time had worsened. On finding Arshan busy, Sanya tells him that she would pay a visit to the local bookstore. Sanya wanted to read some book as she now had the time. She had not picked up a book in months. She was too busy trying to finish her first novel. When she finished writing her book, the book promotion tour took up much of her time. She thought this was the ideal time to read a book. Sanya leaves the hotel and walks to the small bookstore located at the corner of the street, a few feet away from the hotel. Sanya had noticed the bookstore while she and Arshan were arriving at the hotel. Sanya enters the bookstore and is immediately pleased to find her own book displayed amongst those of other author's books. As she enters, Sanya lays her eyes on two other persons in the bookstore. They were engrossed in browsing through the books. One was a young girl, probably a college student dressed in jeans and a jacket who was reading the blurbs of the books. The other was a man in his early thirties, who was searching amongst the books probably for his favourite author's book.

Sanya moves into the bookstore and starts looking at the books. She is so into the books that she does not see the man in the bookstore approach her and stand beside her. " Hello," the man says to Sanya. Sanya looks up at the man with a startled gaze. The man smiles at her and says again," Hello. I am Amit. Aren't you Sanya Wadia, the author?" " Yes, I am," Sanya replies." Well, I have read your book. You have written a wonderful book," said Amit. " Thank you. I am happy that you liked the book." " Do you live here," Amit asked. " No, not actually. I am here on a holiday with my family," Sanya said. " I am also on a holiday," said Amit. Sanya remarks," I haven't read a book for quite some time now. So, I came out in search of a good book to read." " I too am looking for a book to read," Amit said.

Amit Khanna, for that was the name of the man who had accosted Sanya. He told Sanya that he was a major in the Indian Army. He was from New Delhi and had taken leave from his job and had come to Shimla for some relaxation. Sanya stated that she was in Shimla with her husband and her two children. Both Sanya and Amit buy some books and go their separate ways. While walking back to the hotel, Sanya thought to herself that in this age of social media and the proliferation of news channels, everyone who is someone is recognizable. The several interviews that Sanya had given to the news channels and the promotion of her book on social media had definitely made her a very prominent face in the field of literature. Anybody who had an interest in literature would be able to pick her out even in a crowd. Sanya had become that visible.

CHAPTER 26

Amit Khanna is reading the book he bought at the bookstore in Shimla. He is lying in bed and is involved with the characters of the book. But his involvement is superficial as every now and then Sanya's face would rise up in his mind and distract him from his reading. After being distracted again and again, Amit puts the book down and quits his reading. He sits up in his bed and actively visualizes Sanya. Sanya's beautiful face with a childlike innocence that marked that face disturbed him a lot. Amit, when he thought about Sanya, found out that her thoughts not only distracted him but also brought him a lot of pleasurable comfort. Amit had an urge to see Sanya. He thought to himself," If only I could see Sanya again."

Amit Khanna was born and brought up in New Delhi. He had studied in New Delhi till he did his graduation. Then he had joined the Indian Army. His family resided in New Delhi. Amit had got married after he joined the Indian Army. He married a girl chosen by his parents. The incompatibilities of the couple were so glaring from the beginning of the marriage that the marriage had no chances of surviving. The couple had tried to light the spark of love in their married life. But love would not take wings in their life as a couple.

If not love, they thought that if a little understanding towards each other would seep into their lives, it would make life more livable as a couple. But they failed to reach that understanding and a feeling of empathy for each other which would perhaps have saved their marriage. Ultimately after four years of married life, they decided to lead separate lives. They got their divorce.

Amit, now free from an unhappy marriage, wanted to lead a life of solitude with an intermingling of happiness and self indulgence. He had no place for the love of a woman in his life. There had been distractions even when he was encumbered in a marriage. Amit did not shy away from these distractions. He loved women and he loved healthy distractions brought in by women. If the distractions were without the ensuing responsibilities, Amit called them healthy. He never indulged in unhealthy distractions. He was tall and handsome- a perfect mix to attract the fair sex.

The next morning, Arshan and Sanya walk hand in hand through the narrow roads falling in love with the cool atmosphere and the mesmerizing scenery about. They make small talk and move on. Sanya could see Amit Khanna approaching them from the opposite side. As they come near to each other and was about to cross the other, Amit stops and greets Sanya," How are you," " I am fine. Mr. Amit, this is my husband, Arshan. Arshan, this is Amit Khanna. I met him at the bookstore yesterday" Sanya says. Both men shake hands. They were all standing on the road. Amit invites the couple for a cup of coffee at the nearby cafeteria. The three of them take their seats in the cafeteria. Amit sits facing the couple. Sipping coffee, the three of them indulge in chit chat. Amit tells Arshan how well he liked Sanya's book. Amit comes to know that Arshan is an industrialist and that the couple lives in Mumbai. As they talk on, the threesome paints a nice and friendly picture. The only unseemly thing brewing up was in the thoughts that insinuated Amit's mind. Amit every time he saw Sanya seemed to be drawn to her. He just could not keep his thoughts grounded. It flew off to unholy, tainted lands. The fact that Sanya was married did nothing to halt his thoughts and keep them from straying into forbidden avenues. Quite unaware of the working of Amit's mind, the couple spent some more time with him. Then they say their goodbyes and continue on their respective ways. Before leaving, Arshan invites Amit to his home in Mumbai. Arshan had taken a liking to this debonair but somewhat aggressive man. Amit readily accepts the invitation.

Arshan and Sanya spend their days in Shimla by taking rides around the city, by taking short walks and mostly by basking in the warm sun. It was after a long time that they felt a sense of belonging to each other which was otherwise pushed to the background by the other realities of a busy life that both of them led. Their closeness being restored, Arshan and Sanya return to Mumbai. Amit too returns to his home in Delhi.

CHAPTER 27

Meera, Sanya's sister had completed her graduation in Engineering with flying colours. Meera had taken her Engineering degree with Computer Engineering as her speciality. Meera when she surveyed the job market in her hometown of Varanasi found out that there were not many job openings in her field of specialization in her city of birth. This made it necessary for her to move to a city where there are jobs related to the field of Computer Engineering. Meera along with some of her classmates decide to travel to Bangalore in search of jobs to employ themselves in. Meera seeks her parents permission to travel to Bangalore. Her father would have to support her financially till she got a job and got settled in life. Suraj Bharadwaj approves her plan to travel to Bangalore with her classmates. Meera travels to Bangalore with three girls and two boys who were her classmates from Engineering college. The five of them land in Bangalore and put up in a hotel in the city. They search on the internet and find a girls and a boys hostel near to each other. The following day the girls go in search of the hostel. They find the hostel as per their liking and take up rooms in it. Meera takes a single room while her friends decide to share one room. The boys too take up a room in the hostel and decide to share it. The five classmates as they settle in their hostels, also start the arduous task of finding suitable employment for themselves.

After a search of one and half month and after appearing in more than a dozen job interviews Meera finally lands a reasonably good job in a private company. In about a period of one month Meera's classmates too get absorbed in jobs small and big. Their purpose of travelling so far to Bangalore had borne fruit and each of them is successful in their endeavours. Meera joins the company and starts to work. Everyday she would sit in the cubicle allotted to her and wait for the project manager to involve her in any kind of work. But the manager kept her waiting in the sidelines and did not give her any work. Meera started to get restless after a two month period of waiting for work to come by. Meera, when she was bored, would often go and sit by herself in the office canteen and have a cup of coffee. She did not see that all this while she was often being watched by one of the office goers. Ajay Sharma worked in the company in which Meera worked. He had worked in the company for the last two years. He would often see Meera sitting alone and having coffee. One day Ajay thought of introducing himself to Meera and starting up a conversation with her. As Meera has her coffee, Ajay approaches her and greets her," Hello, I am Ajay. I work in this office. May I sit down." Meera looking surprised said, " Yes, Please do sit." " May I know your name?" Ajay asked Meera. " My name is Meera. I joined in the company two months back," Meera answered. Meera came to know that Ajay was from Delhi. Meera told Ajay about her anxiety which was mixed with boredom for not being given any work in this office. Ajay told her not to worry much as it seemed to be the trend in the office that a new entrant would have to wait for sometime before being given any work. Ajay told Meera that he too had to wait a while before he was given any work. He assured Meera that she would soon be given some work to do. Meera felt a lot better after talking to Ajay. Ajay seemed to assuage her fears and make her feel better. He had freed her mind.

In a short span of time since talking to Ajay, Meera was called to the manager's room and was given some work to do. Meera was happy and relieved. She had learnt in these two months as to how hard it was to idle away one's time aimlessly. She vigorously started to develop the software programme she was asked to make. Her partner in developing the programme was a boy named Shirish. As soon as the office hours started both Meera and Shirish would use all their expertise in trying to develop the programme. They worked diligently trying to meet the deadline for completing the work. The manager was very much pleased when they finished their work on time. This meant that new work started to come their way and both of them remained busy. They utilized their time well. Meera and Shirish complemented each other in their skills. Both the partners worked well together. They also became good friends.

Meanwhile Meera's friendship with Ajay had gone beyond the bounds of friendship and had entered the realm of love. The two of them sat in different blocks in the office. As such they did not get much time to converse with each other during work time. But they always had their lunch together at the office canteen. Meera and Ajay did not like to go home and prepare tea for themselves. Both would together have their tea in a small restaurant which was situated opposite to the office. The two lovers would walk out of the office together and would then walk to the restaurant to have tea. This formed their regular habit except on days when either of the two would be absent from office due to ill health. Then each would miss the other very much. On weekends the couple would go out to watch a movie. Sometimes they would visit a park and spend the greater part of the day there munching roasted peanuts and chips. Meera would pack sandwiches for them on these outings and the couple would devour them hungrily at lunch time.

Ajay and Meera were together with each other for one year. They decided at the end of one year of dating that both of them ought to settle together and tie the knot. They decided to tell their parents about their decision when they go home for the Christmas and New Year holidays. The Christmas holidays arrives. Ajay go home to Delhi and Meera return home to Varanasi. Ajay broaches the subject of marriage with Meera in front of his mother. Ajay is close to his mother but not particularly close to his father. Ajay's mother assures him that she would surely talk with his father. Ajay's mother had liked the picture of Meera which Ajay had shown to her. Ajay's father is at first disconcerted at the idea of bringing a girl from another community as a daughter in law into the family. But when his wife insists on guarding her son's happiness, her husband accepts the marriage proposal. Meera lands in Varanasi and goes straight to her home. Meera talks to her father about her relationship with Ajay. She tells him of her decision to marry Ajay. Suraj Bharadwaj inquires about Ajay and his family. Finding Meera to be so much in love with Ajay and finding the boy to be a suitable groom for his daughter, Suraj Bharadwaj agrees to the match. The members of the two families meet in Delhi. Meera's parents, her uncle and aunt travelled to Delhi to meet up with the elders of Ajay's family. It was decided that the marriage of Meera and Ajay would be solemnized in Varanasi in the first week of February. The marriage would be quick and easy. As Meera's parents returned to Varanasi from Delhi, they along with other members of the family start preparations for the marriage. Meera informed her elder sister of her marriage with Ajay. Both sisters Sanya and Meera are excited with the prospect of celebrating the marriage in their hometown of Varanasi. Sanya seeks Arshan's permission to leave for Varanasi some days earlier to the marriage. Arshan allows her to leave for Varanasi two weeks before the marriage. Sanya lands in Varanasi with her children and their governess. Sanya is extremely happy to see her family after a long time.

Arshan arrives for the marriage of his sister in law. He lands in Varanasi on the day of the marriage. The day of the wedding was a happy day for Akash as well. Akash had passed his tenth standard with a good result. The family of the groom arrived in Varanasi four days before the wedding. Then there took place the elaborate ceremonies of mehendi and sangeet before the bride and the groom said the sacred vows and were united in holy matrimony. The bride and groom along with the bridegroom's family took the flight to Delhi the day after the wedding. The rest of Meera's family was left in tears as they bid farewell to their daughter.

CHAPTER 28

Sanya leaves Mumbai for New Delhi to take part in a literary festival held there. She takes her two children with her. Today she is taking part in a discussion on the Indian literary scene along with some authors. The discussion gets over in an hour and Sanya gets up to leave for the hotel she is staying in. As she gets out of the venue and moves to the car, Sanya is greeted by Amit. Sanya is absolutely surprised to see him. Amit reveals that he had come to listen to the discussion. He admits thaat he had come to see her. Sanya is flattered and moved by Amit's admission. She invites him to have lunch with her at the hotel. Amit accepts her invitation and both of them move to the hotel. Farzan and Meher, now over two years old, run to their mother on seeing her. Their governess tell Sanya that the children were on their best behaviour while she was gone. Sanya kisses the children and holds them in an embrace. Amit comes forward and takes the children in his arms, each one in each of his arms. The children being comfortable in his arms giggle out of joy. He kisses them on their cheeks and then puts them down. The two kids, with their governess trailing them, run to their toys to play.

Sanya indicates to the chairs for Amit to sit down. Amit remarks," You have such beautiful children." " Yes, they are like two diamonds in my life," Sanya replied. There is an underlying tension between the two of them. Amit was clear as to where he stood with Sanya. She had been in his thoughts ever since he saw her in Shimla. He wanted a connection with her. He is brash and selfish. All he could think about are the obsessive thoughts of Sanya and that he wants her near him for dispelling those very thoughts. Love was not the emotion that entered his thoughts in any form. It was the compelling need to have Sanya by his side; that was the dominant feeling. Amit consciously thought of moving towards Sanya. It was with this thought that he had come to meet Sanya. Sanya felt a pull towards Amit. He was a new found interest who somehow pulled her towards him. She could not pinpoint what she liked about him; his impudence or his uncanny opinions. He seemed to appeal to her primal instincts. Or these instincts were always present in her and Amit only succeeded in bringing them to the fore. Whatever the reasons, she wanted someone to draw out these instincts. For Sanya, Amit was the person to go to for a realization of these feelings. Amidst the pull of these thoughts, Sanya and Amit have lunch. Sanya shows some nervous energy as if she is not comfortable when she sees off Amit. Amit feels this energy of Sanya and is not unhappy. He feels that he is now one step closer to getting the woman he desires.

Amit invites Sanya for lunch the next day after her programme at the literary festival is over. Sanya agrees to have lunch with him. She looks forward to this meeting with Amit. She is inwardly happy at the prospect of seeing Amit once again. Sanya is a sensible woman. She is herself baffled at the path she would be following if she is to unleash her instincts for this man. It will be a demolition of the life she had created around the love she and Arshan had for each other. But strangely Sanya felt no dilemma over her feelings for

Amit. It was as if she wanted Amit to touch that part of her being that Arshan had not done. Sanya goes off to have lunch with Amit. Amit drives Sanya to a posh restaurant and both of them have lunch. Amit tells Sanya that he had resigned from the Indian army. He was getting ready to open a restaurant in Delhi. He talks to Sanya about his marriage and his divorce. Amit tells her that he had newly acquired a house in Delhi and as such was living no longer with his parents but was living very much on his own. Sanya and Amit are attracted to each other and they feel the attraction growing every minute as they sit talking to each other in the restaurant. Their thoughts are in sync.

After lunch is over, Amit suggests to Sanya that they drop by at his new house. He wanted Sanya to have a look at his house. Amit drives Sanya to his house. It is a two storied building with a little garden in front. The garden is barren waiting for some person to cultivate it. As they enter the house, Sanya could see that much of the house lay empty including the living room, the kitchen and the other rooms. She could see that only a bed and a pair of table and chair had been placed in the bedroom. Amit tells Sanya that he would be purchasing the furniture for the rooms and the crockery for the kitchen soon. He assures Sanya that it will be a decent enough house when Sanya will visit the next time. Sanya laughs and tells Amit that it is fine. She is definitely not judging him on the way the house is at present.

Sanya sits down on the bed after making a tour of the house. She finds the house functional and spacious. Amit comes into the bedroom and as their eyes meet, Amit comes towards Sanya and kneels down in front of her. Taking Sanya's hand into his own, Amit kisses both her hands. He then looks up at Sanya. Sanya smiles back at him. Amit gets up and pulls Sanya up to her feet. He then pulls

Sanya towards him and kisses her on the lips. Sanya loves the way Amit kisses her, first slowly and then with urgency, that she too responds and kisses him back. Amit helps Sanya pull out her sari and as she stands before him in her blouse and petticoat, Amit slowly opens her blouse. Both of them then lie down in bed and make love in the most passionate way. Both are happy in the way things are between them as both discover that they are equally passionate for each other. Amit drives Sanya to the hotel in the evening. They promise to see each other again. They both express their need to continue their rendezvous.

CHAPTER 29

Sanya returns to Mumbai feeling like a teenager with secrets to hide from this world. She feels excitable with a lot of vigor to contend with. She feels amazingly alive. This was the first time that she did not go in search of Arshan on reaching home. She did not feel the urge to call him as she always did when she came home from afar and did not find him at home. She did not think of him at all. The memories of the time that she spent with Amit was all that encompassed her. She felt happy. Without her realizing it, her marriage with Arshan had deteriorated over these couple of years. Arshan being thoroughly busy with his work would forget that Sanya needed his attention most of the time. Sanya was a person who craved for her husband's attention and care all the time. She was inwardly a very insecure person. This insecurity made her to hold on to any person close to her in order to make her feel secure. It was when she felt secure that she felt happy and imbued with a lot of fervour for any activity. It was Arshan's long hours away from his home in England and now in India that made Sanya feel lonely and uncared for. Arshan remained preoccupied with his work even when he was at home. This was the thing which made the situation to deteriorate further. Their closeness every night did little to make

Sanya feel better. When Amit came along, Sanya mistook his longings for love and care.

Arshan recognizes the change Sanya has undergone since her coming back from Delhi. He finds her disinterested in most things at home except perhaps her children whom she loved to distraction. Arshan started to miss the everyday things that Sanya did for him. She would cook dinner for him. She would fuss around him trying to take care of his needs. She would leave whatever she was doing when he came home and would be attentive to him in all the waking hours. He now finds Sanya engrossed in her own work when he reached home. He would find her conversing over the phone for long hours. At night it so happened that he would come to the bedroom and find Sanya asleep most of these days. She seemed not to care for his kisses and caresses. In earlier days she loved to be loved by Arshan in all the ways he wanted to love her. Her disinterest made him sad most of the time. But he loved her so much that he let her be. Her disinterest did not prompt him to love her less. But the love he reserved for her urged him to understand the nature of her disenchantment.

The Wadias are celebrating the eightieth birthday of Parinaaz Wadia in a grand way. They had invited friends and family from India and abroad. Amit was in Mumbai at the time. Sanya tells Arshan that Amit was present in Mumbai. Arshan invites Amit to the party. Sanya is excited at the prospect of seeing Amit again. The long conversations she has had with Amit ever since she came away from Delhi soothed her but she wanted to give vent to the burning desire in her heart. With Amit now close to her, she wanted to go on a journey of giving expression to her desires. The party is in full swing when Amit arrives at the party. Sanya rushes to greet him. " You look beautiful, Sanya," Amit remarks. " I can't tell you how happy I am to see you, Sanya says to Amit. " I can see it. The happiness is written all over your face," Amit says. Arshan sees Amit and comes forward and greets him. He offers him drinks which Amit accepts. As the party proceeds, Sanya loses all her interest in the other guests present in the party. She pays all her attention to Amit and spends most of her time talking to him. This does not go unnoticed by Arshan. It is obvious to him that Sanya is paying an undivided interest to her new found friend. It surprises him as he had known Sanya to keep only a few friends close by. That something might be amiss between the two of them did not enter his mind. He found the friendship between Sanya and Amit a bit unusual but that was all that he thought about it.

Sanya had invited Jennifer and Jacob to the party. Sanya and Jennifer are excited to see each other. Each had so much to share with the other. Sanya especially had a lot to confess to Jennifer. She longed to tell Jennifer of her secret liaison with Amit. She wanted to know what Jennifer thought of it. She decided that this was not the right time or the right place to discuss with Jennifer her affair with Amit. When Amit arrived at the party Sanya introduced him to Jennifer as a very good friend. Jennifer was a bit taken aback by the manner in which Amit's gaze fell on Sanya. It was certainly not the look of a friend but seemed to indicate something else. It was an ardent, passionate look. When Jennifer saw Sanya giving all her undivided attention to Amit, Jennifer was certain that something was brewing up between Sanya and Amit. Jennifer pulls Sanya to the sidelines of the party and demands to know what is happening between Sanya and Amit. Sanya assures her friend that she would tell her everything on another day. Jennifer takes a promise from her friend not to do anything silly.

CHAPTER 30

Amit had come to Mumbai for a couple of days. On meeting Sanya, he decided to defer his departure from Mumbai by another three days. He wanted to meet up with Sanya again. He was staying on in a friend's apartment in Mumbai. His friend was away on a business trip to Dubai. Amit thought that his friend's place would be the best place to meet up with Sanya. Amit asked Sanya to meet him at a particular restaurant in the city. Sanya was happy that Amit was staying back in Mumbai for a few more days which meant that they would spend more moments together. Sanya meets Amit at the restaurant and after having a cup of coffee, they immediately go off to the apartment Amit was staying in. Sanya was a recognizable face in Mumbai, being Arshan's wife and now being a author who had gained some popularity. Sanya had told Amit that their affair if discovered by someone would sooner or later reach Arshan's ears. Sanya at present wanted the affair to be discreet.

Sanya and Amit met in secret at Amit's friend's apartment. After Arshan's departure to office, Sanya would go out to meet Amit. They would make passionate love to each other and lie in each other's arms talking into the evening. Then Sanya would leave for her home. The couple knew that they were being senseless in carrying on an affair which seemed to have no future. But the moments that they spent together were so surreal and there was such an element of suspense thrust into it that they felt more alive. They derived pleasure more from the fact that there was an agenda to be secretive from the world and they found it thrilling to a great extent. They were acting like giddy teenagers. Amit was happy to start this affair with Sanya because he felt it to be a part of one of his so called " healthy distractions". He was happy to have such a lovely woman as Sanya in his arms. Sanya was not in love with Amit. Amit seemed to dispel her insecurities that lay deep inside her. He seemed to make her outward awkwardness which was part of her sense of insecurity vanish in a way that made her face the world with a new attitude. Amit seemed to her to be a breath of fresh air. She however always pictured a home whenever she thought of one as a place with Arshan and her children in it. The picture of a home never included any other person.

Amit leaves Mumbai and goes off to Delhi with a promise to Sanya to meet her soon. After Amit's departure, Sanya for the first time thinks about the future. The first thing that comes to mind is what turn her life will take if Arshan gets to know of her affair. She is for the first time anxious about how he will react. Sanya never ever wanted to hurt Arshan's feelings. He had been a good husband to her. She also could not understand her addictive need for another man's attentions. She failed to understand the working of her own mind. She failed to understand her compulsive need for another's love and attention to make her feel secure. She was just happy when Amit pressed his arms around her and said all the right words. It made her happy. It made her feel confident. It assured her that she was on the right path. But would Amit make a home for her and her children as Arshan had done? She was confused as to what lay ahead for her in the near future. Will this affair mark the end of her marriage?

Arshan was confounded by Sanya's behaviour in recent times. Sanya now remained self absorbed and distant from him. He felt that she did not want to share anything with him. She wanted to remain cocooned in her own thoughts. He was to become aware of why Sanya acted in the way she did in a few days time. A distant relative of his with whom Arshan was close had seen Amit and Sanya entering Amit's friend's apartment. He had seen them continuously for two days. He told Arshan about the incident. Arshan was now amply clear about the reason for the aberration in Sanya's behaviour in recent days. Arshan was angry at first with Sanya. He felt betrayed and jealous. It was his belief that he had loved Sanya sincerely and with devotion. It was this feeling that made the sting of the affair more pernicious. But mixed with the feelings of anger there was also sadness that defined his being. The life he had built up with Sanya seemed to crumble to pieces in front of him. He had always wanted a happy and wholesome life with Sanya and their two children.

CHAPTER 31

Arshan would now stay late at the office and arrive home late at night. Arshan could not think up a way to get out of the terrible mess his life had become. For a time his thoughts were clouded by mixed feelings of anger and failure. Failure in keeping his wife close to him and his family safe from outside influences. After a while Arshan could gather his thoughts together. He thought of saving his marriage and his family from disintegrating. He knew that he still loved Sanya and if she came back to him, he would forgive and forget. He decided to have a talk with Sanya.

Sanya returned home from shopping one evening and found that Arshan had come home early. " You have come home early today," said Sanya when she saw Arshan. " I was waiting for you to return. Can we have a talk?" Arshan asked Sanya. The coldness and purposefulness of those words hit Sanya as unusual. She had never heard Arshan speak to her in that tone and it made her heart skip a beat. She immediately knew that something was not quite right. She sat down in the chair opposite to Arshan. " I know about the two of you. About you and Amit," Arshan said without mincing any words and looking straight into Sanya's eyes. Sanya lowered her eyes being unable to stand Arshan's gaze. She did not say anything but sat still averting Arshan's penetrating look. Arshan continued," Sanya, I cannot let anything or anyone to destroy our family. I cannot let a fling you had with another man to cast a shadow over the beautiful family we have created. I love you. I would forget everything and love you as I have always done. I want you to forget him and come back to me." Sanya tried to fight back the tears that welled up in her eyes. She felt a weight on her heart for the hurt she had caused Arshan. Arshan had always been loving and fair to her. Sanya felt guilty and ashamed. She felt that she was Arshan's wife and the mother of his children and that she had acted irresponsibly. Sanya said nothing. She just kept her head lowered and was tongue tied. Arshan gets up from his chair and comes towards Sanya. He kisses her forehead and walks out of the room.

Sanya cries feeling absolutely lonely and desolate. She sobs for a long time trying to unburden her heart. She is torn between the feelings for the two men that she carries in her heart. She fails to distinguish between the emotions she carries for both men in her heart. Her heart seems to be bursting with all the pain she holds in her heart now. Even after all Arshan had said to her, she was not ready to give up on her relationship with Amit. She was not ready to make a complete break from Amit and come back to Arshan. It was as if the devil had possessed her and clouded her reasoning. Quite unsure of herself she decided to call Amit and have a talk with him. She thought Amit could give her a better perspective on things that intertwined all three of them. She calls Amit and relates to him about the discovery of their affair by Arshan. She tells him about Arshan's appeal to end their affair. Amit in a fiendish way is happy that Arshan had discovered their affair. His convoluted mind found pleasure in the fact that Arshan was anxious and sad with his wife's love affair with him. It made him happy. He now wanted to carry this thrill further by stretching the affair a bit further. It mattered little to him that Sanya will be hurt in the process. He cared little about others. Amit liked that Arshan loved Sanya and that would make the game more interesting to play. Amit tells Sanya to be calm and assures her that he would call her the next day.

Sanya quickly picks up her phone when it rings. The call is from Amit. Amit has come up with an ingenious plan. He tells Sanya to come to Delhi and start living with him. He tell her quite plainly that Arshan could give her security and a stable life but he cannot calm her fears and make her insecurities to go away like he can. Amit tells her to choose between a life which is debilitated by her sense of insecurity and a life of freedom from them. To Sanya's bewildered mind, Amit's proposal seemed sane and attractive. Amit had been able to address her fears in the past and would do so in the future. Sanya chose to lead a fulfilled life. She chose Amit.

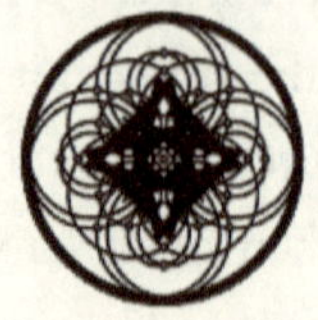

CHAPTER 32

A few days after she received the phone call from Amit, Sanya writes a letter to Arshan, packs her bags and leaves for Delhi at a time when Arshan is busy in office. Sanya is hopeful about the future and as she kisses her children while leaving she is sure that she would in the near future be reunited with them. She and the children would have a wonderful life with Amit. Arshan comes home to find Sanya gone. He reads her letter where she clearly states that she has left him to live with Amit. She states very little else in the letter. Arshan moves around in the bedroom with nervous energy. He is not sure about his next course of action. He paces the room trying to determine his next move. Today Sanya's leaving his house does not anger him but he is rather concerned about her safety. Arshan knows that she had fallen prey to Amit's insinuations. Arshan, when he could think clearly, decides to put in the fight to bring his beloved wife back home. He is determined to keep his heart and his hearth intact.

Sanya in her letter to Arshan writes nothing as to where she would be living. Arshan has a strong inkling that she had gone to Delhi to be with Amit. He knew that Amit lived in Delhi as when they met at the party earlier, Amit had made a passing reference as to the part of Delhi he resided in. Arshan made a great effort to remember Amit's words. When he could finally remember, Arshan decided to take the help of a private detective in Delhi to find out the whereabouts of his wife. He did not go to the police for he felt that it would lead to unnecessary controversy.

Sanya is met by Amit at the Delhi airport and both of them drive to Amit's house. Sanya could see that Amit has decorated his house with the required furniture. It was no longer the empty house that she had found on her earlier visit to the house. Amit brings in Sanya's luggage and asks her to change and take rest. Amit leaves for his restaurant. Sanya is ready to start a new life with Amit. She is happy and settles easily into her life with Amit. Amit is the centre of her life now. He has replaced Arshan as the centerfold of her life. Arshan seemed to have receded into the background as of now. The thoughts of her children often disturbed her. She would then often cry but then she would push her regrets of leaving her children back to her mind as she thought of the future when she would be reunited with her children. Sanya spent most of her time reading and writing. She sometimes cooked for the two of them. She sometimes would accompany Amit to his restaurant and spend the whole day there. She would then mix with the staff in the kitchen and would always have something to say as to the decoration of the restaurant. Meanwhile Arshan has given the responsibility of finding out his wife to a detective in Delhi. He sends Sanya's photograph to him and gives the detective some idea as to where Sanya and Amit might be residing.

The detective immediately starts work on the case. He is very resourceful. He uses his contacts in Delhi to trace out if some person had recently moved into the area as indicated by Arshan. A search ensues stealthily and after a month of unrelenting search, the detective finally spots Amit and Sanya outside Amit's residence. He immediately informs Arshan of the development.

CHAPTER 33

The day Sanya left her home in order to live with Amit, Arshan's world came crashing down. His whole life was turned upside down. He had lost his wife and the children had lost their mother. The wholesome life Arshan and Sanya had created had been destroyed. Arshan's first thoughts were for the children. It would be difficult for the children to cope with life. When Arshan would be away at work, he knew that the children would be safe with their mother. But that being gone now, Arshan knew he would have to fill the space left void by Sanya. He would have to take care of his children as he had not done before. He would have to get more involved with them. Meher and Farzan were two sweet children giving very little trouble to their parents. But the children too were rattled by the absence of their mother at home. They missed their mother thoroughly and would often ask their father about her. Arshan was at a loss as to how to explain about their mother's disappearance. He would often concoct some story to explain the absence of their mother at home. The children missed their mother singing lullabies to put them to sleep and would often cry at bedtime. They would cry till they fell asleep.

Seeing the pain of his children and the pain that seared his own heart, Arshan was more resolved than ever to search for Sanya and bring her back home. He was now certain that he wanted to bring Sanya out of the clutches of that other man. He wanted to resume the normalcy of family life and restore the environment at his home to its pristine days. Arshan sometimes got frustrated with Sanya for leaving him and his home so suddenly. He realized that Sanya might have felt lonely at home without him. But he also thought that Sanya should have spelt out the problems if any to him before taking the final step. She should have let him know if she was unhappy with something at home or with him in anyway. Arshan felt that he deserved to know. He felt that if only Sanya would have told him her reasons of disenchantment, he may have been able to find a solution and thereby prevent the disaster from happening. Arshan was certain that there was definitely some solution to the ills Sanya must have felt in the house or at the most with him. He would have tried to be a good husband. He was sad that Sanya did not allow that and secretly left the house.

Arshan loved Sanya sincerely and wholeheartedly. He would fulfill all that she wished for. He had let her live the way she wanted to live. He had never ever imposed his will on her. So it baffled him when Sanya betrayed him and went away with another man. Arshan thought about Amit and the chameleon he turned out to be. Arshan gets bitter everytime he thought about Amit. He would curse the day he had let Amit into his life. Arshan berated himself for failing to judge Amit's character and his intentions. If he had some inkling of Amit's motives he would surely have warned Sanya. Arshan is angry with himself for not noticing anything amiss in the relationship between Sanya and Amit when he saw them at the party and mistook the relationship for mere friendship. He feels himself a fool now.

Arshan gets angry with Sanya too at times. Arshan always thought Sanya to be an intelligent person. He thought she would be a better judge of people's character. All these thoughts apart, Arshan also knew for sure that if Sanya would come back to him he would accept her with all his heart. He would forgive her and take her back as if she had never left him. His home was hers too. Arshan dismisses all these thoughts from his mind and as he gets information about his wife from the detective, Arshan gets ready to go to Delhi to bring his wife back home. He does not know why he has the confidence that once he finds out Sanya and has a talk with her Sanya would surely come back to him. She would surely come home.

CHAPTER 34

Amit entered Sanya's life and created havoc in it. She had no one to blame but herself for letting Amit into her life and allowing him to destroy the fabric of her peaceful, happy life. Her good friend, Jennifer, sensing something very wrong with the way both Sanya and Amit acted at the party had warned Sanya not to do anything stupid. Jennifer was hinting at Sanya not to do anything to destabilize her marriage with Arshan. Sanya had wanted for some time now to talk to Jennifer about her situation. But she was afraid of Jennifer's reaction and so refrained from talking to her. Jennifer would surely point to Sanya's stupidity and would rebuke her for taking a self destructive route in life. For Jennifer disliked Amit the first time she met him. She had made her opinion quite clear to Sanya. Jennifer had found Amit to be supercilious and manipulative. She did not mince her words when she gave her opinion of Amit to Sanya. As a matter of fact Jennifer was acerbic. She did not think Amit to be a good person. As such Sanya was afraid to tell Jennifer about the step she had taken of leaving Arshan and of being with Amit.

Sanya is filled with a certain feeling of guilt at leaving her children alone at home. The children were so attached to her that they would not leave their mother's side throughout their waking hours. Sanya loved her children deeply. They gave her solace when Arshan was away from home. Whenever she felt lonely she would spend time with the children. She would play with them and at times clutch them to her bosom. They took away a lot of the loneliness Sanya felt. Sanya could not help but compare her situation now with the time when she was with her children. She at times desperately wanted her children with her. She wanted to see them, hold them and love them. They were as much hers as they were Arshans, Sanya knows for sure that Arshan would never allow the children to be taken away from him. Like her he loved them too much. In spite of the circumstances being unfavourable to Sanya, she still hoped against hope that her children would be with her in the near future. She had hope that Amit would definitely help her in keeping the children close to her. For that is what Amit had assured to do for her when he had asked her to come and stay with him in Delhi. But when Sanya came to Delhi and started to live with Amit, Amit seemed to have pushed all the promises he made to Sanya to the background. Sanya sometimes felt that he had completely forgotten about them. For Amit showed no interest or little interest in the things that Sanya was concerned with. Sanya at times felt as if Amit was in the least bit interested in her.

Amit became her whole world when Sanya started to live with him. The thoughts of Arshan was let by Sanya to linger at the back of her mind somewhere and lament there. Like she did with Arshan, Sanya loved to do all those things for Amit too. She would cook for him, look after his clothes and basically look after his comfort at home. Sanya did this with a devotion. Amit was mostly unappreciative of her efforts. What Sanya noticed was that Amit hardly took notice that she took so much care to make him comfortable at home. It was in such moments that Arshan once again crept slowly into Sanya's mind. For Sanya always knew that Arshan liked being looked after by his wife though he did not say it in so many words. Arshan's every gesture showed it to Sanya. Once she left him Sanya pushed off any thoughts of Arshan that threatened to come to the fore and disturb her peace with Amit. She sincerely wanted to be devoted to Amit. Devotion was fine. But was Sanya in love with Amit? Or was she out of love with Arshan? The answer was easy if Sanya looked a little deeper within her being. Arshan still occupied her thoughts everytime Amit was unkind to her in his words or in his deeds. Sanya would recall very clearly the kindness and the care shown to her by Arshan during their courtship and after their marriage. Sanya would remember each word or deed of kindness rendered to her by Arshan. She would remember everything with infinite joy and fondness. She would then know the obvious differences between Arshan and Amit. It was not just these differences or the act of kindness of Arshan that made Sanya remember him. It was also the thrill of his touch and the way he espoused love to her that made Sanya crave for all that she had left behind when she walked out on Arshan. Sanya often lay awake at night and quietly thought about Arshan. This happened often after the act of love with Amit.

CHAPTER 35

Sanya is bitterly confused about her decision to leave Arshan. She was initially very clear and had no doubts about her decision to jeopardize her marriage. She thought she was leaving Arshan for a sane, more wholesome life. Scarce did she know that she was now in the company of a man who loved playing mind games. She slowly and painfully came to the realization that the love and security she craved for was not to be found in Amit. Over the past one month Amit's utter coldness had come to the fore. She started to feel that he was emotionally unavailable most of the time. He was also cruel and unrefined in that he would retort back at some of the opinions she expressed in the most unbecoming manner. Sanya would be aghast at his reactions. He would rebuke her on matters which she always felt were quite inadvertent and did not require such strong reactions from him. She felt that more than protecting her soul, he was bent on destroying it. Sanya felt Amit was not doing it on purpose but that this sort of behaviour was second nature to him. When she talked to him about her children, Amit's reaction was either to turn around the subject or in other times to not to pay any heed to it. He once referring to Arshan remarked with a cruel smile," They are in capable hands. Don't worry." Sanya was aghast and sad. The differences between Arshan and Amit were too glaring for Sanya to see and absorb.

Sanya had always found Arshan genuine and kind hearted. The ruthlessness he displayed in his business dealings were not to be seen when he dealt with the people he loved. Sanya had realized this in their first few meetings. The care and concern he showed towards her made her realize that. Sanya, during her stay with Amit, had realized that she loved Arshan. Amit had not been able to replace the feelings of love that she had for Arshan. Even their physical closeness to each other had not been able to bring Sanya to love Amit. Love had flowed naturally in her heart for Arshan. But try as she might, Sanya felt no love for Amit. She had forced herself to think that she was in love with Amit. The realization that it was not love that she felt for Amit came only lately.

Sanya is bedridden with fever. She lay in bed burning with fever. Amit goes out to the restaurant after tossing some pills at the bedside table and asking Sanya to take them. Sanya on an instinct takes her phone and calls Arshan. Arshan is at his office. When he sees Sanya's number flashing on the phone screen, Arshan immediately picks it up. Arshan cries out," Hello, Sanya. How are you?" Sanya says in a choked voice," I am sick Arshan". Suddenly the line disconnects. There is silence at the other end. Arshan again rings up Sanya's number. He is alarmed when Sanya does not pick up the phone. Arshan decides to immediately leave for Delhi. Arshan, when he got the report from the detective about Sanya's place of residence, had decided to leave for Delhi in a day or two. The phone call from Sanya made this an immediate necessity.

CHAPTER 36

Arshan boards the flight to Delhi as evening comes on and reaches Delhi at nightfall. He goes to the hotel which he had booked earlier and drops his luggage. He then gets on a taxi and gives the driver the address. He is driven through a maze of streets in Delhi. It seems to him that he would never reach his destination. He is a man in a hurry. He is beside himself with worry for Sanya. He feels that Sanya needs urgent help; his help to extricate herself from whatever she was facing. Sanya had also told him that she was sick. He feels alarmed and deeply concerned for Sanya. As he reaches Amit's house, he quickly pays the taxi driver. He rushes to the gate, opens it and goes up a couple of stairs. He rings the doorbell and waits.

As Arshan waits for the door to open, big drops of rain start to fall. Inside the house Amit is busy drinking in the living room while Sanya is down with fever and is lying on bed in the bedroom. As the doorbell rings consistently, Amit letting out a curse walks to the door and opens it. He lets out a sigh as he beholds Arshan. Arshan catches hold of the door and opens it wide. He steps inside and looks around the room. When he could not find Sanya, Arshan asks Amit," Where is Sanya?" Amit laughs and says," I thought you had come to meet me. Sit down and have a drink." " I don't want to talk to you. I have come to take back my wife," Arshan says with clenched teeth" You want the woman who left you without a thought. She will leave you again. You are just not capable of keeping a woman," Amit says. Arshan could not take in the insult. He catches hold of Amit's shirt collar and with force pushes him into a chair. Amit gets up from the chair and staggers ominously towards Arshan. Arshan punches him on the face so hard that Amit falls to the floor. Amit loses consciousness and lies on the floor.

Arshan leaves Amit lying on the floor and goes in search of Sanya. He crosses the living room and enters the bedroom. He finds Sanya lying on the bed. He quickly moves to the bed and finds Sanya asleep. He puts his hand on Sanya's forehead and finds that she is hot with fever. As Arshan touches Sanya's forehead, she opens her eyes. On seeing Arshan, Sanya says," Take me away from here. I want to go home." " Yes dear. I am taking you home." Saying this he goes outside and halts a taxi. Arshan runs inside and lifting Sanya in his arms takes her and puts her gently in the taxi. Arshan instructs the taxi driver to drive them to the hotel he was staying in. With the help of the hotel staff Arshan locates a doctor. He takes Sanya to the doctor. The doctor examines Sanya and gives her the required medicines. The couple spend the night at the hotel. As the morning comes in, Sanya's fever subsides. Arshan spent the better half of the night awake. He could not sleep as he was worried about Sanya's recovery. He constantly kept checking on Sanya.

Sanya gets up from bed and tightly embraces Arshan. Arshan kisses her forehead and says," Let's go home sweetheart." Sanya holds Arshan for a long time. Being held in his arms gives her the comfort of a home. The home she had lost when she looked for it outside his embrace. The couple boarded Arshan's private jet to come back to Mumbai from Delhi. Sanya asked Arshan about their kids with tears in her eyes. Arshan wiping off Sanya's tears said that they had absolutely wonderful children for though they missed their mother a lot during Sanya's absence from home, they had behaved with such grace. Arshan explained to Sanya as to how he had employed a private detective to find out her whereabouts. As the plane lands in Mumbai and the couple make their way to their home, Sanya is joyous. As she opens the door to her house and her children rushes to greet her, Sanya feels her world is complete. She feels as if some missing piece had finally fit into the puzzle.